"The Lord isn't going to let that voice of yours stay hidden. You're hiding your light under a bushel basket, Cora St. Germaine. One of these days He is going to step in and see that it's used for the purpose for which He gave it to you."

—Miss Ida Allen

Savannah Secrets

The Hidden Gate
A Fallen Petal
Double Trouble
Whispering Bells
Where Time Stood Still
The Weight of Years
Willful Transgressions
Season's Meetings
Southern Fried Secrets
The Greatest of These
Patterns of Deception
The Waving Girl
Beneath a Dragon Moon
Garden Variety Crimes
Meant for Good
A Bone to Pick

Savannah Secrets

A Bone
to Pick

KATHLEEN Y'BARBO

Guideposts

Danbury, Connecticut

Cover and interior design by Müllerhaus
Cover illustration by Pierre Droal, represented by Deborah Wolfe, LTD.
Typeset by Aptara, Inc.

Printed and bound in the United States of America
10 9 8 7 6 5 4 3 2 1

A Bone
to Pick

Chapter One

"A party without cake is just a meeting."
Julia Child

IT WAS FINALLY FRIDAY AND the end of the first week of August. Monday would begin the first of two weeks that private investigators Meredith Bellefontaine and Julia Foley had agreed to close down Magnolia Investigations and take a vacation. While Meredith's children were whisking her away on a family trip, Julia had planned absolutely nothing.

That suited her just fine, especially given the news she'd just received via her quarterly retirement fund statement. At the suggestion of their new financial advisor, who'd taken over when their previous advisor retired, she and Beau had made a decision to move their money from lower-earning bonds into a more aggressive portfolio.

That had been four months ago.

Apparently a lot could happen in four months. And it had. Julia sighed.

While they hadn't wanted to live out their final years in luxury, Julia had hoped they could at least maintain their current lifestyle. The numbers staring up at her from the page suggested that lifestyle just might include a massive downsize in living arrangements should she ever think of fully retiring.

"How could this happen?" Julia whispered. "We've worked so hard, and the bottom line is going in the wrong direction."

Meredith stuck her head into Julia's office, her purse slung over her shoulder and a briefcase in her hand. "I thought you'd be gone by now," she said.

Julia glanced up at the clock. "It's not yet three. If I'm taking two weeks off starting on Monday morning, I figure the least I can do is put in a full day's work on the Friday before."

Not that she would be much good for concentrating on work after the bad news she'd received.

"Good for you," Meredith said. "If I didn't have to be fully packed and ready to go by eight o'clock tomorrow morning, I might do the same."

Julia sat back and placed her pen next to the legal pad where she had been making notes. "Eight o'clock? On a Saturday morning? Do you have an early flight?"

"I have no idea," Meredith admitted. "The kids are keeping it all very hush-hush. I was told to pack cowboy boots if I have them. That's a little unsettling."

"I'm sure you'll have a great time, whatever it is you'll be doing." Julia punctuated the statement with a smile she didn't quite feel.

Meredith lingered for a moment. "Okay, what's wrong?" She crossed the distance from the door to take a seat across from Julia.

"Nothing," Julia said, brightening her expression. "Everything is fine. Now go home and get packed, and I want to hear all about your adventure when you return."

Meredith sat back and sighed. "You still have nothing planned for our rare two weeks of vacation time?"

"Not a thing," Julia told her with a genuine smile this time. "I'll enjoy my time with Beau and read several books, I think. I may even cook a few meals. But I'm going to try very hard to do absolutely nothing."

"Nothing?" Meredith lifted one perfectly shaped brow. "No organizing?"

"Well, all right. Maybe I do have a project or two in mind."

Meredith chuckled. "Of course you do. I've never met a more organized woman, and yet I guarantee if I asked you right now which part of your house needs work, you'd have a list."

"Bathroom cabinets, master closet, and that sock drawer I keep ignoring," Julia rattled off. "And let's not even talk about the home office."

They shared a laugh. "Seriously though," Meredith said, "do something fun while you've got this time away. You and I both love our job, but life isn't just about work. Take a few days away with Beau somewhere. Be impulsive, Julia. You might actually like it."

Julia shrugged. "You're right. And I promise I'll do something fun, okay?"

Meredith studied her for a moment and then nodded, apparently satisfied with what she saw. "Okay then." She stood. "I'm off. Pray for me. I'm terrified about what the directive means to bring cowboy boots if I have them."

"It means you're going to have a good time. Now go!"

"I'm going! But promise me you won't stay until five. It's a beautiful day out there. Get your weekend started early."

"If she won't, I will," their assistant, Carmen Lopez, called from her desk in the foyer.

Julia and Meredith laughed. "Go," Julia repeated. "And give my love to the kids."

"I will. See you in two weeks!"

Meredith scooted out of the office, bidding Carmen goodbye, and then the sound of her footsteps receded as she headed toward the back of the grand old home in the historic district where their office was situated. A moment later the back door opened then closed.

Julia looked down at the notes she'd made on her retirement fund statement and sighed. Meredith was right. She had two weeks ahead with absolutely nothing required of her. Staring at the numbers was not going to undo a bad decision and return hard-earned money to their account.

She folded the statement and tucked it into her briefcase then looked around her office. Did she need to take anything with her when she left today?

Carmen's cell phone rang, and she answered. Due to the proximity of Julia's office to Carmen's desk, Julia could hear their assistant's side of phone conversations unless she closed the door. There was no need for that today. No project demanding her attention. So the door remained open, and Carmen's conversation drifted toward her.

"Oh no. Not again. If that dog isn't chewing something up, he's running off. But I'll be watching for him."

There was a pause, and then Carmen spoke again. "About Seth. He's super nice, and I'm not saying that because he's also super rich and offering a reward for Bosco. I mean, sure, a rich boyfriend isn't a bad thing for anyone, but he loves you, Amy. I've seen you two together. Stop worrying. Why don't I come by after work, and we can go out looking? No charge. Unless you've got some of those empanadas left from lunch service. I mean, they are my abuela's recipe."

Apparently, Amy had lots to say. Silence fell for quite some time while Julia rose and collected the things she intended to take home.

"Bosco will show up, probably before I get there. As for Seth, trust your heart," Carmen said. "You know that a man who loves your dog has a leg up on the competition."

A minute later, more laughter bubbled toward Julia from Carmen's desk. "Well, maybe he needs to buy dog training for Bosco. Then he wouldn't eat such a valuable library card. Now don't worry. He'll turn up. In the meantime, I'll pray, okay?"

After a few more minutes of talking, Carmen hung up. Then her chair scraped, and Julia heard her footsteps heading toward the office. She looked up as Carmen stepped inside.

"Has something happened to your friend's dog?" Julia asked.

"You know Amy? She owns Amy's Bistro and Bakery."

"That darling place on Oglethorpe Street near the corner of Drayton? Of course I do. Has she lost that little black dog again?"

"Bosco loves his adventures," Carmen said, resting her arms on the back of the chair Meredith had just vacated. "But this time he was with a dog walker. She took Bosco on that historical tour for pets, which is where the dog walker used to work, and—"

"Hold on a second," Julia interrupted. "A historical tour for pets?"

"Yes," Carmen said. "Woof Walk Historical Tour for Pets. It's a walking tour of the historic district geared toward bringing your pets. Since the dog walker Amy chose once worked for Woof Walk, she trusted her. But I guess Bosco decided he'd rather walk alone."

Julia shook her head. "I hope he comes home soon."

"So do I." Carmen shrugged. "I'll go help her look once I'm off."

"Why don't you go ahead and close up?" Julia suggested. "I'm about to leave, and we're certainly not going to take on any new cases on a Friday afternoon when neither Meredith nor I will be here for two weeks."

"That would be great. Thank you, Julia," Carmen said. "I hope you've got something fun planned."

"You sound like Meredith," Julia said, smiling. "Yes, it will be fun for me, I think. Remember, if anything comes up, I'll just be a phone call away. Call me, not Meredith."

"Will do," Carmen said. "But what could happen?"

Julia groaned. "Never ask that on a Friday afternoon, Carmen!"

They closed up the building together, and then Julia held the back door open for Carmen to exit first, reaching behind her to turn off the kitchen lights. "Enjoy the quiet the next two weeks."

"You too," Carmen said before she climbed into her car and drove away.

That evening Julia held on to her thoughts about the unexpected dip in their retirement funds, thinking over how she would tell Beau the bad news. While he had agreed to the change in investment strategy, she'd been the one who had argued for it.

She went to bed still not sure what to say and spent all of Saturday mulling over the issue. On Sunday morning Meredith called before Julia and Beau left for church.

"I've been spared," her friend declared.

"Oh?" Julia reached to pour her second cup of coffee. "From what?"

"The family vacation," she said. "It's been postponed due to a raging stomach flu that's making its way through my grandchildren—literally."

"Oh no." Julia took her mug to the kitchen table and sat down. "So you're not doing anything on your vacation either?"

"Not if I can help it," Meredith said with a chuckle. "I'm going to try the Julia Foley vacation plan and just enjoy being home."

Julia smiled. "How long do you think that will last, Meredith?"

"You know me too well," she said. "I do have some ideas of how to spend my unexpected free time, but I haven't settled on anything yet. I know I won't be coming in to the office. I promised Quin I'd take an actual vacation, and I will."

They chatted for a few minutes, but Julia couldn't bring herself to seek her friend's advice on how to speak to Beau about the bad news she'd been keeping to herself. By Monday morning, however, she'd almost figured out the right way to approach him.

Then he announced he'd be spending the day running errands. She was relieved to see him drive away, knowing the hour of her reckoning had been postponed.

The phone rang as Julia stepped back inside. It was the office.

Julia checked her watch.

"Good morning, Carmen," she said. "I didn't expect to hear from you before ten o'clock on Monday morning. Is something wrong?"

"Hey, Boss," Carmen said. "There's a ton of messages, and most of them are from Amy's boyfriend, Seth Stevenson. I think something happened. He just kept saying he needed someone from the agency to call him back because it's urgent. I thought I'd let you know that before I call him."

"Was the dog found?"

"Bosco?" She paused. "He hadn't turned up as of last night. Amy's beside herself. Likely that's why he's calling. Oh, sorry. The other line is ringing."

They hung up and then a few minutes later, Carmen called back. "Okay," she said without so much as a greeting. "Seth is adamant that we help find Bosco."

"Since when do we look for runaway dogs?" Julia asked.

"I told him that," Carmen said. "Well, I mean I was nice about it, but he's not taking no for an answer. Do you think maybe you could call him and tell him yourself?" She paused. "Or maybe you could make a tiny exception to your no-work-for-two-weeks policy and take this case on?"

"Why would I do that?" Julia asked. "Meredith and I are a team."

Carmen wasted no time answering. "Of course, but you don't have anything planned, and it would help Amy and probably earn us plenty of free food and an immediate pass to the front of the line anytime we want to eat lunch at her place. You know that's priceless."

Julia chuckled. "As priceless as line jumping at Amy's might be, I want you to call this Seth fellow back and tell him you've given me his messages. Tell him I'll return his call after I've spoken with my partner and considered whether I'm willing to give up my planned vacation time."

Less than five minutes later, Carmen called back. "Uh, Boss, there's been a little unexpected wrinkle and some good news. Which one do you want first?"

"The wrinkle, please," Julia said, dreading whatever it was she was about to hear.

Carmen took a deep breath. "Bosco didn't run away. He was stolen."

"That's not good," Julia said. "What's the good news?"

"In addition to his plan to advertise a big reward on television, radio, and social media, Seth is willing to pay the agency a fortune to find the dognappers and bring Bosco back to Amy."

"How much is a fortune, specifically?"

When Carmen told her, Julia said, "Text me Seth Stevenson's phone number, please."

A few minutes later, she was speaking to the man who desperately wanted his girlfriend's dog returned.

"Thank you for returning my call," Seth said. "I apologize for being such a pest, but I'm determined to find Bosco, and my research says you're the best team for the job."

Julia stifled a chuckle. "I'm not sure where you're getting your research. We've never taken on any lost dog cases."

"No, but you've got an excellent success rate on the cases that you've taken on." Seth paused. "The ones that are public knowledge, that is. Plus, you know Amy."

"Yes, she's really nice," Julia said. "And an excellent cook. So tell me why you believe Amy's dog has been stolen."

"Before I go any further, is it true you can't tell Amy anything we discuss unless I give my permission?"

"That is our policy," she said.

"Okay, great. I don't want her to worry. I've gone over the facts, and they don't add up. Bosco loves to run off, but he always comes back within a few minutes. He adores Amy and would never be gone so long unless someone had him. And as much as that dog loves her, I love her more. Please, won't you help find Bosco?"

Julia felt for the man. The fee he offered was more than generous, but Meredith had promised Quin she would enjoy her time away from work for the next two weeks. Thus, there was only one answer she could give.

"I understand that you're upset, Mr. Stevenson, and I'm terribly sorry. But my partner and I are on vacation this week, so we couldn't possibly take this on."

Then he told her to call him Seth and doubled the amount he was willing to pay.

Even after expenses, her portion would be very close to the amount she had been fretting over ever since she saw the investment statement. She took a deep breath and let it out slowly.

Was this the answer she had been praying for? She could work this case alone, but she would never consider it unless she got Meredith's blessing.

And of course they would still split the fee, either way. Julia would insist.

"I'll have to call and discuss this with my partner."

"Sure, okay, but please let me know soon," Seth said.

"I will." She hung up and dialed Meredith. "I know the answer is no because you've made a promise to Quin not to work for the next two weeks, but you're not going to believe how much I've just been offered for us to look for a lost dog."

"Since when do we look for lost dogs?"

"That's your question?" Julia asked. "Not how much?"

"Okay, how much?" Meredith asked.

Julia told her then hastened to add, "I was actually calling to see what you thought about me taking this. I don't mind working alone, and you would still get half." Then she paused. "Carmen promises we'll be moved to the front of the line at Amy's, but I don't have that in writing yet."

"Honey, sign me up," Meredith said with a laugh. "Have you seen the lines there at lunchtime?"

"Seriously though, what about your promise to Quin?"

"I promised Quin I would take an actual vacation, and I plan to do that. I've been on the phone this morning trying to find a nice beach house on the Outer Banks. I've just heard back from a place that's available starting a week from today. Do you think we can find the dog by then?"

Julia smiled. "If we haven't, I'll finish the job by myself."

"Great. This sounds like an answer to prayer," Meredith said, unwittingly echoing Julia's thoughts.

"I think it might be. Let's find a missing dog." She hung up and called Seth back. "I've spoken with my partner, and Magnolia Investigations would be happy to take your case."

"Excellent," Seth said. "Can you stop by the bistro this afternoon around two thirty? I'll meet you there unless my one o'clock meeting runs long. I've got some great ideas for getting the word out about Bosco. I've already bought some media time and made a sizeable donation to the Police Benevolence Fund."

"Seth," Julia said, "you absolutely cannot bribe the police by making a donation."

"Oh no, it's not a bribe at all. Just a little thank-you for all they do. Besides, the big money is going to be in buying media ads, but I'll fill you in when we meet. Ciao!"

"Ciao," she echoed as she hung up and put her phone away.

Chapter Two

Coraline was in his kitchen.

The *Coraline* who'd appeared with the Boston Symphony Orchestra at Carnegie Hall to sold-out crowds in two performances just last night and who'd received rave reviews in all the newspapers this morning.

Here.

In his kitchen.

Oscar Bryant was no stranger to hosting prosperous men of commerce, presidents, and kings at Oscar's, his Manhattan restaurant, without batting an eye, but the renowned opera singer's presence in his kitchen unnerved him. Perhaps it was the nearness of a woman so elusive that she chose only to use her first name. Or it might be the quiet confidence she had about her as she waved away any help he offered.

No, it was more than that.

While it took the right social connections, months of planning, and a flush bank account to dine at Oscar's, it took *a special amount of gumption to reserve his entire restaurant, including the kitchen, on a Saturday evening.*

Spunk, yes, that was it. The internationally famous singer who went by the single name of Coraline sang like an angel but, most of all, she had spunk.

He glanced over to find her adding flour to the ingredients in a mixing bowl. She didn't use any form of measure that he could see, but rather seemed intent on getting the amount just right by slowly adding spoonfuls as if dusting the ingredients with each item she added.

It was how his mother taught him to cook. Her way was to bypass cups and teaspoons and let the dish being prepared tell him what was needed.

Oscar frowned. He hadn't thought of his mother in years. Her presence in his life, relegated to a safe place in his heart and rarely considered, had formed him. Had given him a love of cooking. Of feeding people.

He missed her terribly when he allowed himself to consider what life had been like with her alive.

Now his father? Yes, he came to mind far too often these days. Mostly when Oscar looked into his mirror while shaving and confronted the image of the man who'd walked away and left a ten-year-old child in the care of an Atlanta piano maker who was looking for an apprentice. While Oscar was no good at the work the piano maker set him to, he learned two things during his time there. First, he could figure out how to do just about anything as long as he was hungry and in need of a warm, dry place to sleep. Then came the second realization. Oscar Bryant was meant for better things, and he wasn't going to find them in Georgia.

Shaking off the thought, Oscar returned his attention to his guest. Thus far since she'd arrived at the alley entrance to his kitchen—her arrival having been arranged through a series of correspondences delivered by messenger early this morning—she'd said nothing beyond the sparest of greetings.

Just a polite hello as she gave his kitchen a cursory glance. Then a nod. That was all. From there she'd set off to do whatever it was she'd wanted to do when she requested he close Oscar's this evening.

Considering what she paid for the opportunity to cook here, Oscar should leave her to it. He should offer a measure of privacy, especially given how notoriously Coraline guarded herself from the press.

But she hadn't asked him to leave, so here he would stay. At least until he was dismissed.

She wore her long, dark hair—glossy chestnut, in his estimation—twisted up into a chignon. Her skin was luminous, though a shade darker than the pale look that the society women who frequented his restaurant preferred. The color in her cheeks made her look as if she'd just come from a long walk.

Perhaps she had.

He'd certainly seen no escort when she arrived. Nothing to show that she had been swept from whatever place she had been hiding to the alley behind his restaurant by carriage or any other sort of conveyance.

Interesting to think that a woman who refused all contact with the press or her fans would walk about so openly. Anyone who passed this beautiful woman on the streets of New York—clad tonight in a dress of shamrock green with her hair caught up beneath a matching hat—would indeed be struck by her unforgettable countenance. However, they would never consider that the lady might be the same elusive opera singer who had held the world in the palm of her hand just last night when she performed.

The only thing Oscar saw in those small but busy hands now was flour, as she'd set the spoon aside and was now using her fingers to perfect whatever she was creating. A strand of hair—now absent of the hat she'd discarded upon arrival in the kitchen—escaped its pins and fell down into her eyes. Absently, she pressed it away with the back of her hand, leaving a smudge of flour across her forehead.

His fingers itched to wipe away that smudge. To return perfection to her face.

He wouldn't, of course. Nor would he move from where he stood, for if he did, she might remember he was there.

Coraline looked up then. Sharply, as if she'd guessed the direction of his thoughts.

"Would you like some help?" Oscar asked quickly to fill the silence.

"No, thank you," was her swift reply.

He nodded, uncomfortable as a schoolboy called on the carpet by the headmaster. "Then I'll just go handle a few pressing matters."

When she went back to her work, Oscar was left to try to figure out what sort of pressing matters might need his attention. He had a chef who ruled over his kitchen and the cooks, a dining room manager who did all the work of keeping the dining room and its staff in tip-top shape, and a business manager who did the remainder of the tasks that kept the restaurant in business.

Somehow in the five years since he'd opened what had become the most successful restaurant in Manhattan—in all of New York City if the newspapers were to be believed—he'd become redundant. He had gone from doing it all to being a figurehead reduced to shaking hands with patrons.

Oscar was good at making acquaintances of strangers and even better at keeping them at arm's length. The habit suited him, even if it had rendered him a thirty-year-old man who went home to an expensive but empty home every night.

He couldn't help but wonder if Coraline did the same thing. If she was as notoriously guarded in her private life as she was publicly.

"Cardamom."

It took him a moment to realize she had spoken, long enough that the meaning of her words escaped him.

Oscar shook his head. "I'm sorry. What did you say?"

The strand of hair had come loose again. This time she blew it out of her face with an upward breath.

"Cardamom," she repeated. "Do you have any?"

Oscar moved closer, gesturing toward the box where his chef kept his spices. "There. I'll get it." He found the jar marked with the spice and moved closer to place it on the worktable in front of her. "Is there anything else?"

For a moment he thought she might not answer. He was about to turn and leave the kitchen when her eyes met his.

"Some company, perhaps?"

Oscar did not hesitate. "Yes, of course. I'll even be your sous chef if you need the help."

"I don't." Coraline paused, her gaze returning to the workspace in front of her as she reached for the jar of cardamom. "But I would like to have it all the same."

Her speaking voice was soft as Southern honey, her expression neutral. Yet something in her eyes...

He walked across the kitchen to reach for an apron from the peg on the wall and then returned to her side, tying it on as he walked. Coraline had declined the offer of an apron before, so he did not make another now. Rather, he stood waiting for his instructions.

"Get the oven ready first," she said.

Coraline told him how hot she wanted the fire to be then went back to her work. Oscar did her bidding like a love-starved pup, only watching her when he was certain she was looking away.

Their hands collided as they both reached for a spoon at the same time. Oscar jerked his back but not before the connection was made.

It seemed as if he'd lost a decade and a half of his life in that instant. He'd been all loose limbs and tied-up tongue at fifteen anytime a female deigned to acknowledge his presence.

Just like now.

Oscar shrugged off the thought. What was wrong with him?

"What are you making, exactly?" he asked to fill the silence.

Coraline glanced up from her work. "A cake."

Emboldened, he continued. "So you just decided you needed to bake a cake, and you picked my kitchen to do it in?"

Coraline appeared to consider the question. Then she lifted one shoulder in a shrug. "I needed to bake a cake. The concierge recommended your kitchen. Are you helping or not?"

"I'm helping," Oscar hastened to say.

Coraline passed the bowl of batter in his direction. "Then stop talking and stir this."

***

Though her host was not a tall man, Oscar Bryant's presence filled the room. Cora supposed this might be because this was his domain. His kingdom.

Mama had been that way. Tiny in size, but once she stepped into her kitchen, little Lottie St. Germaine was the queen of all she surveyed. Cora was missing Mama something fierce today, but all that would be remedied tomorrow when she went home.

Using a clout she rarely called upon, here she stood making the same cake that her mother baked for the rich ladies back home in Savannah before Cora's voice took them away from all that.

The same cake that Mama always made for Cora's birthday, even after they'd been able to purchase the finest sweets any city—or country—had to offer. Then Mama took sick.

Cora sighed. Had it already been three years?

Some days when the routine of rehearsals, performances, and traveling between cities wore her emotions down to numbness, it seemed as though Mama's presence was a long-ago memory. Other times, like here in Oscar's kitchen, it seemed as though she stood just out of sight nodding her approval and urging just a little more cardamom be added to the cake.

Mama did like plenty of cardamom in her cake.

"Just a little more," Cora said, reaching for the jar of Mama's favorite spice.

Oscar continued to stir, not questioning her decision. The control of this kitchen had been transferred to her for the evening. Just one more thing that fame and her improved finances could buy.

If only those things could bring Mama back.

Anyone who had attended Carnegie Hall last night would certainly find it difficult to believe that the woman at center stage accompanied by the Boston Symphony Orchestra would want to be anywhere else. Oh, how she thanked the Lord for His gift of her voice. It truly was a testament to Him that she'd been plucked from the church choir and elevated to such a position.

And yet her heart ached for Mama's kitchen. And soon she would be home again.

She glanced down at the cake batter, and then, waving Oscar away, she reached down to dip her pinky finger into the bowl, tasted the batter. With a nod, she declared it good.

Cora wandered the kitchen's supply room until she found the pans she needed. When she returned, she instructed Oscar on the exacting process of greasing and flouring the pans. Only then did she take over, adding equal parts of the batter to each pan.

Not by measuring but just by looking. Exactly like Mama always did.

Cora allowed Oscar to settle the filled cake pans into the oven. Then silence fell. She hadn't considered this part of the evening. Hire out the restaurant and ask the owner to send his staff home? Yes, she'd done that a few times before, and it was rarely an offer that was turned down. But never had she invited the owner or head chef to stay.

Not until Oscar.

There was something different about Oscar Bryant. Beneath that polished New York veneer was something he thought he was hiding well. A regret, she guessed.

Perhaps it took a person with a secret to recognize one in others.

To be sure, Oscar Bryant was a fellow of good reputation and sound character. Her man who looked into these things had assured her of that. So what was it that lurked just beyond those handsome features?

Just behind that lovely smile?

Oscar moved over to another oven and bent to open it. With his hand wrapped in a length of cloth, he retrieved a platter covered with a cloche then closed the oven again. He returned to his spot beside her and removed the cloche.

"You made dinner?" Cora asked.

"I hope you don't mind. I wasn't sure if you'd want something to eat, or if you'd be making your own meal. The concierge didn't say, and I didn't want to assume." He met her gaze and shrugged. "It's just beef stew with carrots and potatoes. Nothing fancy."

"I see."

His expression remained unreadable, but she could see indecision in his eyes. "All right. I'll stay out of your way," he finally said.

Then her stomach had the audacity to growl. Ever so slightly, Oscar's lip turned up in the beginnings of a smile. She matched his grin.

Then they laughed.

First Oscar brought two stools and then two bowls and spoons. It was, by far, the best birthday meal anyone had ever made for her since Mama.

Perhaps turning twenty wouldn't be so bad after all.

They laughed and talked well into the evening. To Oscar's obvious surprise, she had two bowls of his delicious stew.

"I've always had a good appetite," she told him. "When the food is good, that is."

"I'll take that as a compliment," he told her as their eyes met once again.

Silence fell between them.

"You'll be moving on tomorrow, I suppose," Oscar said, jolting her from the comfort she felt in his presence.

Great pains had been taken to disguise her identity when she purchased the tickets, and she'd told no one of her plans. How could Oscar know?

Cora's surprise must have shown in her face for he hastily added, "I was just thinking if you are still in New York tomorrow, perhaps you and I could have dinner again."

"Oh," she managed on a sharp exhale of breath.

"I'm sorry. That was abrupt. I shouldn't have asked." He retrieved their empty bowls and spoons and took them over to the sink. "This evening has made me forget you're the Coraline and not just a woman I would like to spend more time with."

Her heart warmed to this sweet man. "Oscar, that is possibly the nicest thing anyone has said to me in a very long time."

Oscar turned back to her and laughed. "Then you don't read the papers, because there's not a critic in New York who doesn't love you. They've all said some very nice things."

In truth she hadn't read any newspapers in ten days. The last time she had picked up the New York Times *that had been delivered alongside her afternoon tea—an ordinary Wednesday with sunny skies and absolutely no portent of the heartbreaking news to come—she had read that a train crash at the Park Avenue tunnel had taken the life of seventeen souls and injured more than three dozen more.*

Among the dead was the one man who knew her as Cora St. Germaine who sang at the Methodist church in Savannah, Georgia.

James Peters had been walking past the Wesley Methodist Church on Abercorn Street when her choir solo stopped him in his tracks. To hear Mr. Peters tell it, he'd discovered an angel's voice in the body of a gangly thirteen-year-old.

He was an investor from Boston, a man whose fortune had come from knowing just where to put his money for the best outcome. Mr. Peters—she never called him James, not once—loved the opera and claimed to know a good singer when he heard one.

It took some convincing to get Mama to agree to the grandfatherly man's plan, but eventually the St. Germaine ladies were saying goodbye to Savannah and hello to a world of costume fittings, rehearsals, and concerts all over the world.

Along the way Cora lost Mama—a devastating blow— but she'd always had Mr. Peters to guide her career and keep her steady. Until the eighth of January when he boarded a train and never got off again.

It was a stunning rise to fame, swift and with a singular path that led her to last night's performance at Carnegie Hall. That the orchestra accompanying her at both shows was from Mr. Peters's native Boston made the night all the more fitting as her last performance.

A student of Mr. Peters's ways, she knew when to act, and the time was now.

She would depart tomorrow.

"Coraline?" Oscar asked. "Are you all right?"

"Yes. I'm sorry." Cora shook her head then waved away the direction of her thoughts with a sweep of her hand. "Enough of that. Let's see if that cake is edible or not."

Oscar nodded. "Right. If it's as tasty as it smells, then I'm sure it is."

He followed her to where the cake was cooling on a rack. "I haven't missed that you didn't answer me about where you'll be tomorrow. I apologize if that question was too personal. You're rumored to prefer your privacy."

Cora looked up into Oscar's eyes. For a moment she weighed the option of postponing the plans she'd made to disappear from this life to return to the one that had been calling her since Mama passed on. If anyone was worth remaining for, even if only for a short while, it just might be Oscar Bryant.

And then the moment passed. No, she could never be normal again. Not until she stopped being the international sensation named Coraline and returned to being just plain Cora St. Germaine from Savannah, Georgia.

Maybe she would even rejoin the choir at the church.

Mr. Peters had insisted that in order to make her famous he would need to make her background a mystery. Thus, Mama told her friends and neighbors that she and Cora were going to start a new life in Boston. The why of it was never addressed.

"Unlike most of the rumors about me, that one regarding my privacy is true," she told him. "Now, would you do the

honors and cut the cake? I don't think I can wait another minute to taste it."

He smiled. "I'd be happy to, but on one condition."

Cora gave him a sideways look. "What's that?"

"Next time you make dinner, and I'll bring dessert."

She laughed. Of course there would be no next time, but it was easy to pretend there might be.

"All right, but I'll need that stew recipe."

Oscar shook his head. "Oh no you don't. You come up with the menu. But I'll be sure to bring the recipe along with dessert." He held out his hand. "Shake on it?"

After a moment's hesitation, Cora extended her hand. "It's a deal, Mr. Bryant."

"Oh no," he said. "It's Oscar. Anything else is too formal for someone you've got dinner plans with."

"Dinner plans," Cora said even as she knew there was no future for them. "That may or may not happen," she felt obligated to add.

"We shook on it, Coraline." Then he laughed. "Don't worry. I understand. You're a busy woman. I just feel like someday we'll find each other again and we'll have that dinner."

Cora smiled. "And I'll get that stew recipe."

Chapter Three

AMY'S BISTRO AND BAKERY FILLED the first floor of a building last owned by the Pettigrew family. Heirs to a fortune in old money, the Pettigrew sisters—Lena and Mabel—bought the home on Oglethorpe Street sometime around the middle of the last century. They remodeled it in the style of a Victorian castle complete with stained-glass windows depicting the family crest they had created for the occasion.

Twenty years of remodeling followed another twenty of the Pettigrew sisters becoming the cream of the Savannah social crop from the 1960s through the 1980s. Unfortunately, neither survived to welcome in the new century, nor did they make any sort of arrangements for what would happen to the place after they were gone.

Since then, the stately structure had been bought and sold, abandoned, remade into a rooming house for the less fortunate, and then ultimately left abandoned again. When Amy Bryant arrived in Savannah to attend the reading of a will belonging to a long-lost relative two years ago, she became the building's current owner.

Meredith had learned all of this from her connections at the historical society and gleefully explained it to Julia over the phone on the way there. Apparently those folks were serious about their old buildings, serious enough to make sure they knew just who owned what and what the owner planned to do with it.

Julia gave thanks that she had a partner who knew people who could offer the shortcut version of the history of just about any house, church, statue, or park in the city. Sometimes it wasn't what you knew but who that would break a case wide open.

Julia smiled as she pulled into a coveted parallel parking spot within sight of Amy's Bistro and Bakery. Oglethorpe Street was filled with its usual traffic, but other than the occasional pedestrian, the crowds were not present just yet on the sidewalk. But then it was too early for dinner at Sooz's, the French restaurant next door, and Amy's Bistro and Bakery was closed on Mondays.

She turned off the engine and unbuckled her seat belt. Meredith was not here yet, at least as far as Julia could tell, but Julia had arrived early.

Rather than sit and wait, she decided to get out and walk around. Perhaps she might see something that caught her attention and would lead to a clue. After working with Meredith at Magnolia Investigations for as long as she had, Julia knew that information might come from the least likely of places.

Oglethorpe was a wide avenue divided by a tree-lined center filled with azaleas and other plants that bloomed in the spring. While many of the buildings on this street had been converted for commercial use, others were still used as homes. Some were in their original condition as a single-family dwelling while others were split into duplexes or apartments.

Just as with other places in this part of Savannah, the eclectic mix was part of its charm. And, considering there was a missing dog, it could also be part of the problem. Bosco could be anywhere in this area. As she glanced around, Julia was acutely aware of the fact that there were many places where a small dog could be hidden. Too many.

She spied Carl Flynt, the letter carrier who delivered mail to the office, deep in conversation with a young blond woman. He looked up when she approached and offered a smile, though concern was etched on his usually jovial face.

"Afternoon, Judge," he called.

No matter how many times she asked him to simply call her Julia, he never quite managed it. Rather, he insisted on using the name he'd used when his former route had been the courthouse.

"Good afternoon, Carl." She looked to the woman and offered a smile.

"This is my niece, Stephanie Sterling." He paused to look down at his companion. "Stephanie, this is Judge Julia Foley."

"Hello, Stephanie," Julia said. "Actually I'm a retired judge. Now I'm a private investigator at Magnolia Investigations."

The woman's smile matched hers, but there was no happiness in her eyes. "Pleased to meet you."

Julia had obviously interrupted an important conversation. "Pleased to meet you as well." She looked to Carl. "I hope Carmen has warned you that she's got a large mailing going out in a few days. Something she's going to be working on for a charity she's involved with."

Carl chuckled. "She told me all about it. Said she had permission to work on it while you all were out of the office, and she was worried the boxes might be too heavy for me. She offered to help, but I won't let her. I may be old, but I'm not so old that I can't carry boxes of mail to my truck. I thought I'd wait and see just how many she's got. Likely I can find some strong young fellow to help who might need the exercise."

Julia laughed. "You're probably right."

"I can see how Carmen could convince a fellow to flex his muscles and help," he said. "She's a spirited young woman, but then I like that. My Ed is that way, and it keeps me on my toes."

Edwina "Ed" Porter, a retired FBI agent, was Carl's fiancée. They'd been engaged as long as Julia had known the pair, which had been at least ten years, and neither of them seemed in a hurry to plan a wedding.

"We're blessed to have Carmen working for us," Julia said. "And speaking of working, do you have a minute to answer a question?"

"I'll leave you two to your conversation. I need to get going." Stephanie hugged Carl then bade Julia goodbye.

Carl watched her go before turning back to Julia. "I worry about that girl. There's always something with her. But you don't need to hear about all that. What did you want to ask me?"

"There's a dog missing from this street—a little black schnauzer. I'm curious if you might have seen him on your route."

"Amy's dog," he said. "I did hear Bosco was missing, but no, I haven't seen him. I'd have noticed even if I hadn't seen the signs. That little fellow sure does like barking at me from that upstairs window."

"Has he ever tried to harm you?"

Carl shook his head. "No way. Cute little guy, and his bark is much worse than his bite. Plus he wasn't ever out unless he was on a leash."

His smile faltered. Then he shifted his mail sack. "Well, best be getting on."

"Thank you, Carl. You'll let Amy know if you catch sight of him? Or you can call Magnolia Investigations and let us know." She reached into her purse and handed him her card. "If you get voice mail, leave a message."

"Sure will." Carl tucked the card into his pocket then removed his cap and scratched his head. "I sure hope Amy finds him. I know she's missing him something awful. She's been baking cookies and muffins and everything else since then, over and above what the store sells. Says that's what she does when she's upset. Ed told me I'm going to have to buy new uniform pants unless Amy finds that dog."

Julia smiled and glanced at her watch. "I've got to go. It was good seeing you, Carl."

"You too, Judge," he called as she walked away.

Julia made her way down the cobblestone sidewalk until she reached the bistro. She was about to knock when she heard someone call her name.

She turned to look next door where Suzanne "Sooz" Winter stood on the porch of her restaurant with a copper watering can perched over one of the massive hanging ferns that decorated both ends of the space. Tall, thin, and elegant, Sooz wore a long top of flowing white linen over matching white linen pants. From where she stood, Julia could see the chunky turquoise necklace that completed the ensemble.

"Afternoon, Julia. Are you here to make reservations for dinner?" Sooz called. "I'm almost filled up this evening, but I can always squeeze you and Beau in."

"Thank you," she said, "but not today."

"Soon then?" Sooz asked.

"Yes, absolutely," Julia told her.

When Sooz nodded and continued watering her plants, Julia turned her attention to her destination. Though the building still bore signs of its former purpose as a family home, Amy's addition of a frill of green-striped awnings above the front windows and the deep scarlet of the door had given the old girl new life.

Yellow butterflies danced around the profusion of flowers that spilled from the planter boxes beneath the windows. A matching flower basket secured to the door had attracted more of them.

Even the old stone mounting box, a remnant of the days when homes provided a stone step-up just for the purpose of climbing onto your horse, had been covered in blooming plants.

A poster with a photograph of an adorable black schnauzer wearing a peppermint-striped bow tie and Santa hat was prominently displayed above the flower basket and on both windows. Each had the same plea beneath the picture:

PLEASE bring Bosco home! Free meals at Amy's Bistro for life in exchange for information leading to my sweetie's return. And $$$ too! Call, text, or email the bakery with tips.

Julia tried the door, expecting it to be locked. Instead, she found it open and stepped inside to the sound of jingling bells. The sweet cinnamon sugar smell of something delicious baking mingled with the scent of fresh bread to lull her farther in.

To her left, the parlor, with its marble fireplace and stained-glass window depicting the Pettigrew family crest, had been filled with tables covered in red-checked tablecloths awaiting tomorrow's diners.

The afternoon sun danced across a polished hardwood floor that once welcomed visitors to the home. Overhead, the family's crystal chandelier illuminated a space now filled with glass cases where Amy's baked goods were showcased when the bistro was open. Behind the cases, a Julia Child quote proclaimed that a party without a cake was just a meeting.

Julia grinned. Amy's love of all things Julia Child had come to light in a news story documenting Seth's gift of a recently found recipe card belonging to the famous chef. KSAV, a Savannah television station, got wind of the local man's win of the rare collectible at a Wentworth-Townes Auction event in Connecticut. In order to bring attention to his lady love's newly opened business, he allowed a reporter to document the presentation of the recipe card to Amy.

The result was that Amy got lots of free promotion for her bistro and eventually a trip to New York City when the network picked up the story for its Valentine's Day show.

"Hey, Jules," Meredith called, stepping inside behind her. "Sorry I'm late. I had to park all the way down on Abercorn, and then I had to wait for the man ahead of me to figure out how to use the parking meter."

"Those things can be tricky," Julia said.

"Maybe so, but it might've been nice not to have to wait while he tried to find his credit card. Turned out his wife was carrying his wallet in her purse. Can you imagine Beau having you carry his wallet?"

Julia chuckled. "I think not, but then I married an independent man."

"I'm in the kitchen, ladies," Amy called out. "Would you mind locking the door behind you? I had it open for y'all."

Meredith reached behind her to do as Amy asked, and then they followed her voice past the empty display cases and down the hall into the kitchen. Unlike the remainder of the first floor, where Amy left the historic features mostly intact, the kitchen was a gleaming modern space where the only nods to the past were in the black-and-white-checked tile floor and the tomato-red 1950s-era Chambers cookstove.

The owner of Amy's Bistro and Bakery stood behind a stainless steel prep table long enough to park a Buick on. The table's gleaming surface had been dusted with flour on one end, and Amy was rolling out what looked like sugar cookie dough.

Her glossy auburn hair was piled up in a messy bun that appeared to be held in place by a pair of chopsticks. She wore a denim chef's coat over a pair of jeans with pink sneakers. A frilly rose-covered apron that looked as if it came off a 1950s housewife completed the look.

"Thank you so much for coming so quickly and for taking this case," she said, looking up from her work then nodding to several racks of oversized cinnamon rolls cooling on the counter to her left. "I'm worried sick about Bosco. I bake when I'm stressed."

"They smell delicious," Meredith said.

"I'll box some up for you. There's plenty." She sighed. "If I don't get my little pup back soon, there will be enough to feed the entire city. I'm making sugar cookies now. I'll throw some of those in the box too."

"Thank you. It smells wonderful. About Bosco, I have to be honest, Amy," Julia said. "Finding a lost dog is not the usual sort of case that Magnolia Investigations takes on. However, Seth was persistent."

She smiled and looked away. Her already rosy cheeks became a deeper shade of scarlet.

"I'm sure he was. Seth is a very generous man." Amy pressed away a tendril of hair from her face, smearing her forehead with flour in the process. "He's crazy about Bosco too. He had just bought Bosco a new collar the day he went missing. He told me to wait until he got there to open the package, but I'm not one to leave a box unopened—Mama had to hide my Christmas presents when I was a child—so I tore into it as soon as it was delivered. And I couldn't help but put it on my sweet pup. He looked so handsome." She paused but only for a second. "I'm rambling, I know. I'm sorry."

"Don't be sorry, honey," Julia said as an idea occurred to her. Seth had plenty of money. Perhaps he had given her a collar that had drawn a thief's attention. "Amy, describe the collar Seth gave you."

"It was red with tiny black dots, about an inch wide. Seth knows I love red on Bosco."

"Was there anything special about it?" Julia continued. "Something that might make a thief want to take your dog in order to steal his collar?"

She frowned. "I can't imagine what that might be. It was the cutest thing, absolutely. It had a little charm with Bosco's name on it, but it was tiny and probably not worth a whole lot. In fact, the collar I took off him was probably worth more."

"Why?" Meredith asked.

"It's a one-of-a-kind. Bosco tries them out for the collar designer. He's—"

A dog barked, and Julia looked around. The barking continued.

Amy reached for a little plastic schnauzer on the counter and pushed a button on its belly. The barking ceased immediately.

"Isn't that the cutest thing?" Meredith asked. "What's it for?"

"That's the timer for the last batch of cinnamon rolls," Amy told her. "If you don't mind grabbing the pot holders and pulling them out, I'll go get the collar I took off Bosco so you can see it yourself."

Julia and Meredith set to work retrieving a half-dozen pans of cinnamon rolls and placing them on the counter beside the others. Just as Meredith placed the last pan on the counter, Amy returned with a fire-engine-red collar.

She handed it to Meredith. After a moment, Meredith passed it to Julia.

Though she inspected the collar carefully, she could see nothing remarkable about it and said so to Amy.

"It's the little things," Amy said. "Like the padding and the soft lining. Apparently it's some fancy sherpa something or other. It's supposed to be more comfortable around the dog's neck. And the buckle there is lightweight and…"

Amy seemed to run out of words as she shook her head. "I'm sorry. I'm just so upset, and seeing this collar—I've kept it in a drawer since he went missing on Friday."

"I know this is difficult," Meredith said, "but we're exploring every angle."

"And I appreciate it." Amy took in a shuddering breath then exhaled. "My poor Bosco. I hope he bites whoever took him. He's never been a biter, you know. He's got such a sweet, gentle soul. Still…" She dissolved into sniffles and reached for a dish towel.

"We're going to find Bosco," Meredith said. "Are you up to answering more questions?"

Amy looked down at the dish towel in her hands. Black schnauzers marched across the hem, each wearing a different color bow tie. "Yes, but we're going to need a warm cinnamon roll and a glass of iced tea."

Julia's stomach growled. In truth, the cinnamon rolls did smell delicious, and she hadn't had much of a lunch thanks to her worries about other things. A glance at Meredith told Julia that her partner wasn't going to turn down the treat either.

Amy placed a plate of cinnamon rolls on a tray then added a pitcher of iced tea from the refrigerator along with three glasses filled with ice cubes. After grabbing silverware and napkins, she picked up the tray and motioned for Meredith and Julia to follow her into the dining room.

Amy settled them at a table in front of the window that looked out onto Oglethorpe Street. "Okay, what do you want to know?"

Chapter Four

"Is Seth coming?" Julia asked. "I'd like to get his insights too."

Amy placed cinnamon rolls on plates and passed one to each of the ladies then helped herself to the last one. "He planned to, but I got a text from him right before y'all arrived saying his meeting was running long, and he had someone from KSAV waiting to speak to him next about setting up an interview with me."

"All right," Julia said. "Tell me who would want to harm Bosco."

"No one," Amy said. "He's a sweet little guy."

Meredith cut a bite out of her cinnamon roll and paused. "Has he ever bitten anyone or acted threatening?"

"Never," she said with a shake of her head.

"No complaints about him from neighbors? Maybe barking too much?" Julia asked.

"Bosco is a watchdog in an eleven-pound body. During the day he stays upstairs in the apartment, and if I'm gone too long he gets antsy and starts barking at anything he sees—or anything he thinks he sees. He likes to sit in the front window and guard the street."

Julia chuckled. "I can't imagine he would be too frightening."

She smiled. "He's not. But now that the bistro has gotten so popular, I haven't been able to slip away to check on him as much. I worried about leaving him alone too long. He tends to chew on things."

"Like what?" Meredith asked.

"A few weeks ago, he ate a library card Seth bought for me. I was devastated, of course. It belonged to Julia."

Amy paused a moment then continued.

"Julia Child, that is. I'm a huge fan. Seth is so sweet. He must have paid a fortune for that card. But what does he do? He goes and buys a recipe card that belonged to her and surprises me with it. I couldn't let anything happen to the recipe card. That's why I hired a dog walker. I thought I was doing the right thing...."

Julia made a mental note to ask about the recipe card later. Right now her concern was to establish the chain of events leading up to the dog's disappearance.

"I know what Seth has told us, but I would like for you to tell us what happened in your own words," Meredith said.

"Bosco was with a dog walker when he disappeared. Woof Walk came highly recommended." Amy paused to wipe her tears with her napkin then continued. "I paid extra for them to send someone over to walk Bosco alone since I wasn't sure how he would do with other dogs on his first time out."

"Probably a wise idea," Meredith offered.

"I thought so too. He can be a little feisty when he's stressed."

"So can I," Meredith quipped.

"But Stephanie did a great job with him, so we continued to use her. Anyway, they said this had never happened before," Amy said.

"What exactly happened?" Julia asked. "Be as specific as you can, please."

"Apparently everything was fine until Bosco got away from her at Chippewa Square. She chased him down Perry Street but lost him when he ducked into Old Settlers Cemetery. That's all I know."

"Who is she? The dog walker, I mean," Meredith asked. "Stephanie who?"

"Her name is Stephanie Sterling," Amy said on an exhale of breath. "I just don't understand. It's not like walking a dog takes a massive amount of training. You hold on to the leash and walk. She never had any problems walking him before."

Stephanie Sterling. The young woman Julia had just met on her way to the bistro. Why hadn't Carl said something when they discussed the missing dog? She would have to ask him that very important question very soon.

She pushed her plate aside, tucked a strand of hair behind her ear, and retrieved a pen and notebook from her bag. After turning to a fresh page, Julia wrote Carl's name. Under it she added *talk to him about Stephanie Sterling.* Then she returned her attention to Amy.

"What else can you tell me about the day Bosco disappeared?"

"It had been such a good day. The morning was busy as usual, but we got a delivery that I had to sign for. I took care of that then saw it was from Seth, so I checked in on my staff and made sure that they had everything under control. I went upstairs to the apartment to open the box and check on Bosco."

"And the dog was fine?" Meredith asked.

"Yes, I found him sitting in the front window barking at the delivery driver. Silly dog was so busy worrying about the nonthreat down on the street that he didn't even hear me opening the door."

Julia grinned. There was a lesson in that somewhere about paying attention to the right things and ignoring those that were less important.

"So I played with him for a few minutes—he loves to play catch with his tennis ball—then I gave him a puppy treat and opened the box." Amy paused.

"And then you found the new collar?" Meredith asked. "This cinnamon roll is delicious, by the way."

"Thank you. And yes," Amy said with a shrug. "I took off the old collar and put the new one on him immediately. It looked so good on him."

"Then you went back downstairs to the bistro?" Julia asked.

She nodded. "I worked the rest of the lunch rush, and Stephanie showed up at three thirty to get Bosco. That's the last time I spoke with her before she called to let me know what happened."

"Could she explain how she lost the dog so easily?" Meredith asked. "It seems to me that a small dog like Bosco that's dragging a leash behind him wouldn't be hard to catch."

Amy shook her head. "All I've heard is that Bosco got away. No explanation of how except to say that he pulled his leash from her hand. I mean, how does that happen? You're a dog walker. You have one job. Hold on to the leash." She exhaled. "I'm sorry."

Meredith took a sip of tea then put the glass back down on the table. "No need to apologize. I agree, it does seem odd that she let the leash go."

"I suspect she's covering up for something," Amy said, her words terse.

"Like what? Do you think she took Bosco?" Julia asked.

"I don't know what to think." She shook her head again. "No, I think she wasn't paying attention to my dog at all. Maybe she was on her phone or talking to someone. Worst-case scenario is that she was in on the dognapping, but I don't want to make that allegation without any proof."

"Of course not. Meredith and I will speak with her and her boss and see what we can find out," Julia said. "Is there anything else you can tell us about the incident?"

"I thought I would get help from the police, but they weren't interested in a missing dog. Apparently they limit their canine investigations to known thefts—which mine wasn't at that time—or cruelty cases. Thank goodness I wasn't reporting that."

"Yes, absolutely," Meredith said as Julia nodded. "So they did nothing?"

"Oh, an officer came out and spoke to me. He asked a few questions and went around to speak to my neighbors. Apparently Mrs. Winter wasn't happy about the police showing up during her Friday evening dinner service prep. She let me know about it."

Julia and Meredith exchanged glances. Then Julia returned her attention to Amy. "Is there animosity between you and Mrs. Winter?"

"There wasn't at first," Amy said. "She was very sweet and welcomed me to the neighborhood. The flower basket on the front door was a gift from her, as were a few other things. We got to be good friends. Then the bistro took off, people were lining up to get in, and parking spaces were at a premium. She didn't appreciate that so much."

"And how did you become aware of this?" Meredith asked.

"She told me so," Amy said. "Nicely, of course, but she was very clear that the popularity of Amy's Bistro and Bakery had cut into her profit margin. She even asked me if my landlord knew I had put up awnings and painted the door. I think she was planning to get me in trouble in the hopes I would get closed down. You should have seen her face when I told her the building was mine and paid for—just in case she decided to go to the bank and complain to them."

Julia made a note of this. "What did Mrs. Winter think of Bosco?"

"Once I got him, I don't think she minded him living next door. He never did his business on her lawn or anything like that, and his visits always seemed to be appreciated. We were good neighbors."

"I'm sure you were," Meredith said. "But did he bark at her customers or do anything that might irritate her? I'm sure he was let out in the backyard on occasion. Maybe she didn't like him being out there?"

"He was," she said, "and you're right, Sooz didn't like it when Bosco was in the yard." She looked away as if deep in thought. "Bosco liked to dig, and there was this one place in the garden that was his favorite. If I wasn't careful, he'd dig just enough to get under the fence and end up over at Sooz's place. He loved it over there in her back garden. He would bark at her parakeets, though. That's what got him in trouble with her in the first place."

"That would be annoying to her, I'm sure."

"You would think. Except a couple of times when I was upstairs and I'd let Bosco out to play, I would catch him after he'd already dug under. I tried to keep a close eye on him, but things happen, you know?"

"Of course," Julia said gently. "Go on."

"Well, I would see Sooz out there petting Bosco or playing with him. It was like she enjoyed him being there, but then she would complain when I came to get him. Said she didn't want him around because he was 'too boisterous.'" Amy made air quotes as she rolled her eyes. "Anyway, I just sort of tried to make peace. And to be fair, she was always bringing me new collars for him to try out."

"Why?" Julia and Meredith asked in unison.

"She said it was good for her nephew's business. He's the one who makes the custom dog collars, so anytime he had a new design she would ask me if she could try it out on Bosco. I agreed because I figured it would be the neighborly thing to do. Plus they were always cute collars."

Amy took a sip of her iced tea then continued. "She asked me what color I like best, and I told her I preferred him in red. After that when she would bring a new one over, they were always red."

"How often would she bring a new collar?" Meredith asked.

"It varied. Sometimes it would be a couple of weeks and other times it might be a month or more."

Julia looked down at the cinnamon roll on her plate. Though her stomach growled, she realized she hadn't taken a single bite. She quickly remedied that. "Oh, Amy," she said, "this is delicious."

The young woman grinned. "It's a family recipe," she said.

"There's something special in it, but I can't put my finger on it," Julia said.

Meredith nodded. "I was thinking the same thing. Dare we ask you to tell us your secret ingredient?"

Amy laughed. "I won't swear you to secrecy, but it would be nice if you didn't tell anyone."

"Of course," Julia said as Meredith nodded in agreement.

"Cardamom," Amy told them.

"Really?" Meredith said. "I would never have thought of that."

Julia took another bite just as someone knocked at the front door.

Amy frowned. "I'm not open on Mondays. I can't imagine who would be knocking."

Another series of knocks sounded.

She rose. "Excuse me. I'll go find out." A moment later she returned with a confused expression and a large brown envelope in her hand.

"Is something wrong?" Julia asked.

Amy handed her the envelope. "That was a process server. Seth is being sued."

"Why serve you then?" Julia asked.

"I have no idea."

Julia took the papers from the envelope and skimmed them. "Apparently the attorney for the plaintiff, a man named Phillip Weber, is including you as the person known to be in possession of the item in question." She folded the pleading and then looked up at Amy. "Were you expecting this?"

"I knew there was some controversy over the Julia Child recipe card. Seth bought it at an auction held by the estate of the previous owner. The auction was on the up-and-up. Everything was done right. The lawyer for the estate signed all the right papers. All of that…oh, I don't know the terms, but anyway, it was a legal sale. Then some guy comes out of the woodwork and says he's an heir of that estate and no one asked him if it was okay to sell the recipe card."

Probate cases were messy at best. Julia had presided over a few where heirs had behaved in the same way.

Meredith toyed with the rim of her tea glass then looked over at Julia. "Has Phillip Weber contacted you or Seth directly since you became aware of this issue?"

"No," Amy said. "Seth has been handling all of that. Well, his lawyers have. They said we have nothing to worry about. Something about the heir not having any standing to sue or something." She looked down at the papers on the table between them. "So much for that, I guess, because he's certainly suing."

"The fact he's filed suit doesn't mean he has the standing to sue." Julia gave Meredith a sideways look then returned her attention to Amy. "It looks like Phillip Weber just got added to our suspect list."

"Do you think he took Bosco?" Amy asked.

"Anything is possible," Meredith said. "But there are other possibilities, and we plan to check them all out."

"According to these documents, he lives in Connecticut." Julia met Meredith's gaze then looked over at Amy. "That doesn't mean that he might not have hired someone to do it."

Julia moved to hand the documents back to Amy, but Amy put up her hands to wave her away. "I don't want those. Give them to Seth."

"He should have received a copy. In order to sue, the plaintiff has to make sure all defendants are properly served." Julia put the papers back into the envelope and tucked them into her bag. "We plan to speak to Seth as soon as possible, but we'll take these to look them over."

"Okay." Amy sighed. "I sort of thought this would happen even though the lawyers kept telling Seth it wouldn't."

"Why did you think that?" Meredith asked.

"Seth has this guy working for him named Kenton Hollis. They've been friends since high school, and now Kenton is his accountant. But he's really more than just the numbers guy, because Seth trusts him completely."

Julia heard doubt in Amy's voice. "Do you?"

Amy shrugged. "He takes care of Seth's business and he's Seth's friend."

"That's not an answer to my question," Julia said.

"I don't have any real reason not to," Amy said. "Seth trusts him, and I suppose that's good enough for me."

"Okay," Meredith said. "Then tell me this. Do you and Kenton get along well?"

"In front of Seth we do," she said on an exhale of breath. "But I get the distinct impression he doesn't like me."

Julia shook her head. "Why? Have you given him any reason not to like you?"

"Every day I'm with Seth is one more reason." She frowned. "Until I came along, Seth and Kenton were best buddies. Suddenly Kenton's buddy is hanging out with me and not him. It's no more than that, I think."

"Do you think he took Bosco, Amy?" Meredith asked.

She seemed to consider the question for a moment as she poked at the remains of her cinnamon roll with her fork. Then her movements stilled.

"Don't tell Seth this, but if I had to name names, I would put Kenton Hollis at the top of my list of potential dognappers, although he's smart enough to have someone else do it for him. He may even have urged that guy to sue us about the recipe card. It would be like him to do something that would make me return a gift that Seth gave me."

"Because he doesn't like you?" Meredith probed.

"Because he doesn't like Seth's attention being divided. He actually told me that. I cause Seth's attention to be divided. A man with his intellectual gifts should be concentrating on saving the world, not spending time with a baker." She shook her head. "Anyway, talk to him and you'll hear all of those things and more."

"We will," Julia said. "Now how about we finish up these amazing cinnamon rolls then perhaps take a peek at your apartment before we go? I'd like to see where Bosco lived, if you don't mind."

"Where he lives," Amy corrected, bringing the statement into the present tense. "I say that because I know you'll find him and bring him home. And sure, I don't mind showing you my apartment, as long as you don't mind overlooking my less than perfect housekeeping. I've had a lot on my mind."

"I'm sure it's fine," Meredith said. "You'd be surprised what Julia and I have seen in the course of our investigations. And if you've decorated your apartment like you've decorated your shop, then I'm sure it's darling, no matter what."

"Thank you. And you're right. It could be worse. At least my apartment isn't a crime scene." She stabbed a piece of cinnamon roll and lifted it halfway to her mouth then froze. "Oh."

"What is it?" Julia asked her.

Tears swam in Amy's eyes. "My apartment isn't a crime scene, but my poor Bosco is still out there somewhere." She looked up at them, her expression pleading. "Please bring him home to me."

Chapter Five

JULIA AND MEREDITH SAID GOODBYE to Amy then strolled down Oglethorpe Street toward where they had parked their cars. "Well?" Meredith asked as Julia dug in her purse for her keys. "Thoughts?"

She grasped her key ring and gave it a tug to release it from beneath the other contents of her bag. "Without speaking to the dog walker to get her story, I find it suspicious that she just let the leash go and lost the dog. The park isn't that big, and neither is Bosco."

Julia paused to give the question more thought. Then she continued. "I also found it odd that Amy didn't seem all that bothered by the fact she'd just been served with a lawsuit. I know she said it wasn't a surprise, but on top of losing your dog, you get sued? That's upsetting, to say the least."

"I noticed that," Meredith said. "And she didn't want to keep the documents. All of it was just a little too much. Something's not right about that."

Julia leaned against her car and pushed a strand of hair away from her face. "Maybe she's an avoider. We both know people who would rather pretend everything's okay than deal with what's wrong."

Meredith shrugged. "Maybe. But losing a dog isn't pleasant, and she wasn't avoiding the grief of that."

"True." Julia shifted positions. "I'm glad to have a copy of the suit for our files though."

The door to Amy's Bakery and Bistro opened, and Amy appeared on the sidewalk. "Good," she called. "You're still here. You forgot your cinnamon rolls. I'll just go grab them."

They groaned in unison.

"Carmen will be happy to see those," Meredith said.

"She can have them. If I brought them home, Beau and I would finish them off in no time and then regret it terribly." She joined Meredith in her laughter then sobered. "Is Chase still staying at your place?" Julia asked. "Because I think you need to take some to him."

"Yes, but just until tomorrow. He's alternating between eating me out of house and home and staying up playing video games only to sleep until noon. It's like having a high schooler again."

"But you love it," Julia supplied.

"I do." Meredith's smile was wistful. "Having the boys ten years apart meant I was almost done raising the first one by the time the second one was old enough to start giving me fits. It makes no sense, but I loved every minute of the mess, the broken windows, and high food bills, so yes, I am enjoying a brief return to that."

"Minus any broken windows," Julia added as Amy stepped out onto the sidewalk balancing a stack of pastry boxes in one hand and a large brown bag in the other. "What in the world is she giving us?"

"More to the point, what isn't she giving us?" Meredith asked with a laugh as she hurried to Amy to relieve her of the boxes. Julia followed a step behind to take the bag.

"Okay so I might have gone overboard on the sweets and bread," Amy said. "But I couldn't just give you cinnamon rolls, so there's an assortment." She glanced over at the bag in Julia's arms. "And because I believe in life balance, I also put in strawberry, feta, and balsamic salads for you both and Carmen. If you don't want them for dinner, they'll keep until lunch tomorrow." She made a face. "Oh no, I didn't think about your husband, Julia. Let me go back and grab another salad."

"No, don't do that," Julia hurried to say. "You've done enough. I'll be having this delicious salad for lunch tomorrow, so Beau will never see it."

"If you're sure," she said.

They shared hugs and thanks, then the ladies departed for the office. Julia made a pit stop along the way to pick up a much-needed Diet Dr Pepper. By the time she arrived at the office at half past four, Carmen and Meredith were in the kitchen sharing a cinnamon roll.

"I couldn't let her eat one alone," Meredith said with a giggle.

Carmen grinned. "She's making the ultimate sacrifice. Thank you, Meredith. Oh, this is good. Or as my mama used to say, *muy delicioso.*"

"My pleasure." Meredith popped another bite in her mouth. "Muy delicioso indeed."

Julia chuckled as she set her drink on the counter and opened the refrigerator door. "I'll just put these salads in the fridge for later. Did anything interesting happen while we were gone, Carmen?"

"There was a call from Seth Stevenson. He apologized for having to miss the meeting with you guys and wants to schedule a time when he can see you. I booked the appointment for tomorrow morning at eight." She cringed. "I know that's early, but apparently this guy is hard to get a meeting with. Be glad I didn't accept his first option."

"What was that?" Meredith asked.

"You could have joined him on his five o'clock run at the McQueen Island Rails to Trails running trail."

"That's a three-mile run," Meredith said with a groan. "Unlike you, I do not have aspirations of running a 5K. I'm still in awe that you ran one. Imagine trying to have a meeting with someone while you're also trying not to have a heart attack."

"Not funny," Julia told her.

Meredith had survived a heart attack not so long ago. Though she was in excellent shape now, Julia still wasn't ready for a joke on the subject.

"Imagine trying to have a meeting before daylight was my first thought," Carmen said.

"You mean he was talking about the five o'clock that comes in the morning?" Meredith asked. "Oh, please, no."

"That's the one." Carmen shrugged. "Notice I didn't have to ask if you wanted that option. Besides, it's supposed to storm tomorrow."

Julia cringed. She wasn't fond of storms. "You chose well," she told Carmen. "Now I'm going to choose to go to my office with my Diet Dr Pepper and read over some paperwork, because if I stay here a moment longer I'll be diving into one of those boxes."

"It's not just cinnamon rolls," Carmen said. "Amy threw in a little bit of everything. I just love her."

"How long have you known Amy?" Julia asked Carmen as she paused in the doorway.

"Since right after I came to Savannah," Carmen said. "We met at the grocery store, of all things. I was looking at the frozen dinners, and Amy buzzed by then backpedaled and told me I could make a meal that tasted better and promised it wouldn't take much longer than heating up something frozen."

Julia nodded and took a sip of her drink. "I would agree."

"I'm sure I made some smart aleck comment," Carmen continued. "All I remember is that Amy laughed and said she would prove it. She wrote out a recipe for spaghetti and meatballs on the back of a copy of Bosco's AKC registration while I stood there. I still use it."

"Bosco's AKC registration?" Julia asked. "That's an odd thing to give you, don't you think?"

Carmen shrugged. "I asked Amy that, actually. She said she'd accidentally made too many copies when she was filling out the paperwork to register him in her name—apparently the copy order got changed from one to ten—so she was using them for scratch paper."

The front door chimed. Carmen put her fork down and went to see who had arrived.

Julia took the opportunity to escape to her office, where she settled behind her desk. She slipped her purse off her shoulder and retrieved the envelope Amy had given her then placed the bag on the floor beside her.

She'd almost finished reading the pleadings when the ringtone she used for Beau's calls rose from the depths of her purse. Scrambling to find her phone, she managed to catch the call just before it would have gone to voice mail.

"Sorry," she said. "The phone was in my purse."

Silence.

"Beau? Are you there?"

"Yes, I'm here. Are you busy right now?" he asked.

"I'm reading pleadings," she told him. "But I've got plenty of time to talk to you. What's up?"

"I would rather talk to you about it in person. See you in a few minutes."

Julia placed the phone on her desk and closed her eyes as she sighed. A glance at the time told her it was nearly five thirty.

There was only one explanation for Beau's surprise visit to the office. He'd found out about their retirement account.

She opened her eyes and leaned back in her chair. "I should have told him," she whispered.

It had been her intention to tell him on Friday evening, but they'd ended up having such a nice dinner on the deck, and it seemed a pity to ruin a beautiful night. Then Beau went fishing on Saturday and stayed out most of the day. By the time he returned he was hot, tired, and sunburned. Definitely not the time to tell him bad news.

Since then she'd found excuse after excuse to remain mum on the issue, not the least of which was the unexpected windfall that would replace what was lost by the aggressive investment strategy that Julia had convinced Beau to approve.

It wasn't like her to keep things from Beau, and none of it sat well. Thus, when she heard the front door open and Carmen call out a welcome, remorse had fallen heavy and so had more than a few tears.

Julia snatched up a tissue and wiped her face. She put on a dash of powder from the compact in her desk drawer. Anything Beau had to say would be deserved, but she didn't have to greet him with a splotched face.

When Beau appeared in the door, she blurted out, "I'm sorry I didn't tell you sooner."

His smile fell. "Tell me what, Julia?"

Not the response she expected. Julia frowned.

Beau took a step inside the office to reveal the paper-wrapped bouquet of yellow floribunda roses he had been hiding behind his back. "I saw these Julia Child roses at the garden center around the corner while I was there getting ant killer, and I thought it would be nice if I brought them to you at the office. That's why I called to make sure you hadn't already left for home. And before you ask, I knew the name of them because I read the tag." He paused and his expression turned solemn. "Why did you think I was here?"

"We've got cinnamon rolls in the kitchen," Carmen called out as she walked by. "And just about everything else that Amy's Bistro and Bakery serves, including salad. Help yourself!"

"Thanks, but I'll pass for now," Beau said without taking his eyes off Julia.

Silence fell between them. Once Carmen had retreated to the kitchen, Julia sighed. "Come in and close the door, please." Then she rose and walked toward him. "The roses are beautiful. Thank you."

He remained in place as she closed the distance between them. "Julia?" he asked. "What happened? Just tell me."

She looked up at the man she loved with all her heart as more tears threatened. "It was my fault, and I take full responsibility for it. And before I tell you the worst part, let me tell you the best. See, we have a new case and ironically there's a Julia Child element to it, though the case itself is about a missing dog. Anyway, the fee for this new case is substantial—well more than anything we've ever received for a case—so that's the good news, but—"

"Julia," he interrupted, "you're talking a lot but not really making a point. Can I guess what this is about?" At her nod, Beau continued. "You saw the investment statement."

Again, Julia nodded. She might have continued her apology, but the words stuck in her throat.

"And that's what has you so upset?"

Another nod. More words she couldn't manage to say.

Beau pressed past her to deposit the roses on her desk. Then he turned around to face her, his expression as somber as hers.

"I love you so much, Julia Foley."

"And I love you too, but—"

"Nope." He motioned for her to come to him then enveloped her in his arms. "That's it. No qualifications. I love you and you love me. We're in this together."

"But I shouldn't have convinced you that the aggressive strategy—"

He halted her words with a kiss. When they parted, Julia smiled. "You certainly know how to win an argument with me. Not that we were arguing, but you know what I mean."

Beau shrugged. "Anytime, Mrs. Foley."

Julia laughed and then shook her head. "Seriously though. I feel awful about what happened to the investment account."

"So do I." Beau gave her a sideways look. "That's why I brought you flowers. I was afraid you would see the report from the brokerage and blame me for suggesting we stay with the same firm after our guy retired."

"So you came here to bribe me with roses?"

"Not bribe," Beau said. "The bribe happens when you get home. I've made my famous potato salad to go with the fish I'm planning to cook on the grill."

Julia rubbed her hands in anticipation. Beau had made his potato salad for their very first date all those years ago, and he knew it was still her favorite.

He looked down at his feet then back up to meet Julia's gaze with a shrug. "We're a fine pair, aren't we? I blamed myself, and you blamed yourself, and we're both worried about the other one's feelings."

She grinned. "I think you just summed up the ingredients of a good marriage."

His smiled broadened. "I think I might have mentioned this before, but I love you, Julia Foley."

"You might have," she said, reaching up on tiptoe to give him another kiss. "But you can say it as much as you want, and I'll never get tired of it."

There was a knock at the door. "Julia? Are you still here?"

She took a step back from Beau and smoothed her hair back. "Yes, Carmen. Come in."

The door opened, and Carmen took a step inside. Then she faltered. "Oh, was I interrupting anything?"

"Actually, I was just leaving." Beau's attention never moved from Julia's face. "I'm making a special dinner for my wife tonight." He reached out to grasp her hand and then made his way out of the office and down the hall.

Carmen grinned. "Couple goals," she said. "You two are adorable."

Julia chuckled. "Did you want something, Carmen? Since it's after five I thought you'd have gone home by now."

"Oh right. Yes. Before Meredith left she volunteered Chase to help with my charity boxes, so I called him. He's going to come over now and help me assemble them in the conference room if that's okay."

"Sure," she said. "Just lock the doors while you're here and make sure he walks you to your car if it's after dark when you leave."

"Will do," Carmen said as she hurried away. "I'll call him now to tell him it's okay," she called over her shoulder.

Julia went back to her desk and the Julia Child roses that Beau had brought her, then turned her eyes heavenward. "You really blessed me with that one, Lord. Thank You."

A moment later, the front door opened again. "Julia?" Beau called as he hurried up the hallway. "Aren't y'all looking for a little black dog?"

She hurried from her office. "A black schnauzer, probably ten or twelve pounds, wearing a red collar. Why?"

He nodded toward the open front door. "I just saw one run past me heading toward Forsyth Park."

Julia snatched up her phone and purse and hurried outside with Beau. "Where were you when you saw him?"

"The entrance to the back lot was blocked by a delivery truck, so I had to circle around to find a parking space down Hall Street. The little dog streaked past me on the sidewalk heading toward the park."

Forsyth Park was the largest park in town. Between the tourists who came to see the famed fountain and the locals who populated the benches and green spaces, the place would be crowded even on a hot August evening.

"Was anyone chasing him?"

"Not that I could see."

"Okay," she said as she tried to formulate a plan. "Beau, if you'll drive around the park and see if you can find him, I'll go after him on foot in hopes someone has seen him. His name is Bosco, and it wouldn't hurt to call him as you drive."

He gave her a doubtful look. "I'm thinking that might be awkward, honey."

"It might be," Julia said, "but it also might solve this case."

Beau sighed. "Bosco?" At her nod he shrugged. "I'll see what I can do. I'll call you as soon as I've made it all the way around."

"Thank you," she called as she turned to race toward the park, grateful she'd worn comfortable shoes today. Ten minutes later her phone rang.

"Please tell me you found him, Beau."

"Sorry, honey," he said. "I didn't."

Her shoulders slumped. She had run up and down the main walkways of the park calling for the dog and attracting the attention of a few animal lovers who were willing to take her card in case they spied him.

"Want me to park and help you look for him on foot?" Beau asked.

"No," she said with a sigh. "But thank you. Could you keep a lookout for him on your way home? He could be running around in a nearby neighborhood."

"Generally if there's a dog running loose, dogs that are penned up behind a fence will bark. Do you hear anything like that?"

Julia paused to listen. "I hear traffic, people talking, and the fountain splashing. But I'll drive home with my windows down just in case I can hear something."

She talked to Beau most of the way back to the office to get her car. As she stepped into the parking lot, she spied an unfamiliar car. Chase must have gotten a new vehicle.

Since Carmen was in the office alone—unless the car was Chase's—Julia quietly let herself into the back door to make sure. She had not yet allowed the door to close behind her when she heard the laughter.

After easing the door shut, Julia walked through the kitchen and followed the sound to the conference room, where she found Carmen and Chase looking at something on a cell phone. Carmen looked up as Julia paused in the doorway.

"Oh hey, I didn't hear you come back in," Carmen said. "We're watching a video, so I guess that's why I didn't hear the door chime."

"Hey, Aunt Julia," Chase said. "I saw you in the park."

"Hi, Chase. I didn't recognize your car, so I figured I'd better come in and be sure everything was all right." She nodded. "And yes, Beau thought he saw the dog that we're looking for running in that direction, so I went to look for him."

"He saw Bosco?" Carmen asked. "Really? When?"

"About fifteen minutes ago. He came in and told me the dog ran past him on Hill Street heading toward Forsyth Park. I didn't think to call for you to help us look," Julia said. "We both looked—me on foot and him in his car—but if it was Bosco, which we're not certain it was, then he's every bit as fast as the dog walker told Amy he was when she let go of that leash."

"Man," Chase said. "I hope you find him. I'll watch for him on my way to Mom's place."

"Thank you." Julia returned Chase's smile then focused her attention on Carmen. "I'll just leave the two of you to your work. Chase, don't let Carmen stay here late, and please see that she gets in her car safely."

"Will do," he said as Carmen rolled her eyes.

"Okay, well good luck with getting these boxes filled." Julia turned and retraced her steps to her car. Just before the door closed behind her, laughter rose again from inside. Then she heard dogs barking in the distance.

Chapter Six

THE NEXT MORNING JULIA ARRIVED at the Manger Building on Johnson Square at five minutes to eight. The weather was warm and sunny in spite of the forecaster's predictions of storms. Though she'd driven around the neighborhood for a full half hour after she left the office yesterday, she never did manage to find any clues as to the whereabouts of the little canine escapee.

After the meeting, she planned to make another sweep of the neighborhood just to make sure. Maybe she would take another stroll through Forsyth Park as well.

After entering the lobby by the massive front doors, Julia walked past a matched pair of palm trees situated beneath an oversized gold chandelier to reach the elevator. As she pressed the button to go up to the penthouse suite, she heard a man calling for her to wait for him.

She turned around to see Seth Stevenson, dressed in black running pants, neon yellow sneakers, and a red T-shirt bearing the logo of Amy's Bistro and Bakery, hurrying toward her. Though she'd seen him interviewed on television several times, Seth looked more friendly and approachable in person than he did on screen. He lifted a hand to wave, and she returned the gesture.

Seth's sun-streaked blond hair was still damp, and he held a white bag in his hand. Anyone who didn't know that this fellow was worth a fortune would likely mistake him for a college kid heading for class.

"Hold the elevator," he called just before he arrived at her side and the doors opened. "I'm Seth, and I'm hoping you're either Julia or Meredith."

"I'm Julia. Meredith called to convey her apologies. She walked outside this morning to a flat tire, so she's handling that instead of joining us."

"Bummer." As they stepped inside, he shifted the backpack hanging from one shoulder and nodded to the bag. "It's Taco Tuesday at the food truck down the street. I hope you're not a vegetarian."

"I assure you there's no danger of that," Julia said as she looked over to realize there was no button to push to indicate that the elevator should take them to the top floor. Instead, there was a small black square next to the number for that floor.

Seth swiped his phone over the small black square, and the elevator set off. "A perk of having the whole top floor to myself," he said with a shrug.

The elevator doors opened, and Seth let Julia precede him. The walls in the vestibule were papered in a deep hunter green and covered with nineteenth-century paintings of Savannah that would have looked at home in one of Savannah's statelier homes.

While Julia was no expert on antique furniture, she recognized the massive mahogany desk that had been placed at the center of the foyer as being both old and expensive. The chair behind it was covered in a lush green tufted velvet that matched the walls. Other than a few well-placed books on the city's architecture artfully placed on one corner and topped by a small bronze version of Sylvia Shaw Judson's iconic statue *Bird Girl*, there was nothing to show that anyone actually used the desk on a regular basis.

"Come with me." Seth nodded toward what appeared to be a blank wall behind him then pressed against the wall and a door opened. Julia cast one more glance around and hurried to follow him.

When she stepped through the door, Julia's pace faltered. In stark contrast to the front part of the office, this space was shockingly open, its walls exposed of their brick and the ceilings removed to show the rafters above. The floor beneath her feet was old wood, its age showing in a patina that could only be developed over time.

Julia was amazed. It was like going down the rabbit hole and arriving in a different place and time.

She took two more steps and froze. The view of Savannah from where she stood was almost three hundred sixty degrees and dizzying given the fact the floor-to-ceiling windows offered no indication of exterior walls. Only the small lobby behind her and the elevator shaft kept the vista from being visible in all directions.

Groupings of furniture—some clustered around television screens hanging from the ceiling and others in the form of desks or tables—were spaced around the room. Each was anchored by rugs that likely cost more than her car. In the far corner, a basketball hoop was anchored to a brick pillar. On the other side of the room, lights from a row of old-fashioned pinball machines flashed and flickered.

Seth turned back to smile. "Happens every time. Come on in and sit down so we can talk."

He nodded to a round metal and glass table with a view across Savannah to the river and indicated for her to sit across from him. After placing the bag on the table, Seth shrugged out of his backpack and placed it on the floor.

"Hang on a sec. I'll get plates." He hurried over to a sideboard that Julia would swear she'd seen an exact copy of at the Savannah Museum then returned with a tray bearing napkins, plates, and utensils as well as various sauces.

After reciting the types of breakfast tacos he'd purchased, Seth invited her to take her pick. "Thank you," she said once she'd made her choice, "but you didn't have to go to all this trouble."

"It's Taco Tuesday," Seth said with a shrug. "It's what we do here."

Julia looked around then back at her host.

He smiled as he opened the wrapper on a bacon, avocado, and sweet potato breakfast taco. "You're wondering who *we* is?"

"I'm wondering a lot of things," she said. "But yes, this is a big space for just one person."

Seth shrugged. "My company isn't bound by location. If my employees want to come in and work here, great. They're welcome to do that. Most choose to work remotely. Some show up every day. It just depends." His gaze scanned the room. "I'm usually the first one here. It wasn't intentional, but I seem to have hired mostly night owls. They'll come wandering in for tacos in an hour or two. Any other day I might not see anyone until the afternoon."

"Interesting." She nodded to the door through which she had followed Seth. "What about the receptionist?"

"We don't have one." At her astonished expression, Seth continued. "I set that area up as a precaution. If someone manages to get past the elevator protocol—say if they jump in the elevator after one of my employees has activated the car to take him or her to this floor—then when that employee leaves the elevator all they see is a reception area that looks like your average high-end Savannah firm."

"Unless they follow the employee through the door. Then it's more like the Bat Cave. Or whatever a place this exceptional could be called."

"Unless it's me opening the door, the employee has a retina scan before the latch is released. A temperature mechanism will alert the system to more than one body in the room, which is another set of security protocols. Beyond that, I won't elaborate. Suffice it to say, the odds of someone coming in here that I don't want in are practically nil."

"That is an impressive level of security," Julia said.

"It's necessary," Seth said, then he shook his head. "But you didn't come here to talk about my business. Have you made any progress in finding Bosco?" He held up his hand as if to ward off an answer. "And I fully expect there hasn't been progress, because you just got the case yesterday."

"Actually, there was something," she said. "My husband saw a dog fitting Bosco's description running up Hill Street toward Forsyth Park yesterday afternoon. Unfortunately, the dog got away and hasn't been spotted again."

"With a red collar?" he asked.

"That's what Beau said."

Seth leaned back in his chair and exhaled, closing his eyes. A moment later, he opened them again. "Okay, so that's progress. It's possible that Bosco has escaped his kidnappers and is loose. Now we just have to hope he turns up."

"Meredith and I will be actively searching for him," she said. "We won't be waiting around."

He smiled. "Good answer."

"We spoke to Amy at length yesterday. She's distraught, as you know, and she gave me these papers. She was served with them yesterday but asked me to take them. I thought it best I give them to you since I knew we were meeting this morning. Just so you know, I made a copy for our files."

Julia slid the pleadings pertaining to the lawsuit across the table toward Seth. He glanced down then back up at her, his expression unreadable.

"I was served too. If Amy doesn't want those, I'll take them. Kenton handles all this stuff. I'll give them to him when he gets in." Seth collected the papers and stuffed them into his backpack then reached for another taco. "Anyway, I'm sure you've got questions for me."

"I do." Julia dug into her bag and retrieved her notebook. "The first one is pretty simple. Who do you think took Bosco?"

Seth laughed. "Simple but difficult. If I knew, I wouldn't have insisted Amy hire you."

"And I wouldn't be here if I didn't think you could give me a list of names to investigate."

"Right." Seth's expression sobered. "Well, okay. You can start with the guy who's suing Amy and me over that recipe card I bought. You're a former judge, so I'm sure you've read the pleadings. The guy has no standing according to my lawyers. He wasn't named as executor and didn't challenge the sale until after it was completed. Pretty much it's a frivolous suit."

"Do you know Phillip Weber?"

"No." Seth let out a long breath. "No, I don't know him. I knew of him, yes, but his name wasn't known to me until the papers arrived and I read them."

"How did you know of him?"

"My lawyers spoke to his lawyers, I think. Generally there are conversations before anything gets this far. I offered to settle for a nice sum, but apparently this Weber guy didn't want to settle. He had to have that card back. All or nothing. Then he gets nothing, I told them. No way would I hurt Amy by taking back a gift I gave her."

When he spoke of Amy, his expression changed. If ever there was a look of love, Seth Stevenson had it.

"Can you think of anyone else?"

"The woman who owns the restaurant next to Amy's place." He shrugged. "She isn't too fond of Bosco. I think she's jealous of Amy's success. I wouldn't put it past her to take him." He paused. "Though she could be a nice lady and I've got it all wrong."

"We're working on that. I also know about the woman who let Bosco's leash go in the park." Julia turned the page until she found the name she was looking for then returned her attention to Seth. "Stephanie Sterling. Do you know her?"

"No. My associate Kenton checked her out and found she's had lots of jobs, although she's somehow managed to stick with this one for about eighteen months. The walking service has an excellent rating, and from what I've been able to determine, nothing like this has happened to them before."

"What about the owner?" Julia asked. "Have you spoken to him?"

"Amy did right after it happened. I thought about following up, but she asked me not to." He leaned back in his chair and ran one hand through his hair. "She knows me well enough to know I might end up giving him what for about upsetting Amy by being so irresponsible with Bosco."

"I'll be speaking to him," she said.

"Good. He controlled the situation that resulted in losing the dog."

"Well," Julia said, "that's certainly something to consider. Does anyone else come to mind?"

"I'm sure you've thought of the ones I could mention," he said.

"What about someone who might be after you because of your business or your financial status?"

"Then you'd have a pretty long list. I'm not in this to make friends, although I think I do a pretty good job of maintaining a good reputation. I don't have any sworn enemies, if that's what you mean. There aren't any other lawsuits pending—at least none that I know of, although we've fought off a couple of patent issues since I started this company."

"Could you give me the information on those?"

"Sure, I'll have Kenton do that when he gets in. Is email okay?"

"Yes, thank you." She paused. "What about neighbors, former friends, old girlfriends? I'm thinking someone in your personal life who has an ax to grind in regard to you. Does that call up any names?"

Seth laughed. "Oh wow. Well, it's funny you asked that because just one name comes to mind. It's this guy I went to high school with. His name is Dan Bell, and man, he hated me. Like absolutely hated me."

"Why?" she asked as she wrote Dan Bell's name on her list. "What did you do to him?"

"More like what wouldn't I do? I wouldn't let him cheat off me, so he failed precalculus and physics his senior year. Because of that he became ineligible to play football. He blamed me for not getting any college scholarship offers. According to Dan, he would be in the NFL right now if I'd just given him the answers to those tests."

Julia's brows rose. "Surely he doesn't still hold a grudge? You're not old, but I'm guessing high school wasn't that recent."

"Ten years ago," he said. "We had a reunion a couple of months ago. Dan was there. Suffice it to say he's still the same."

"Wow, okay. Did he make any threats when you saw him?"

"Just the usual," Seth said with a chuckle that held no humor. "He told me to watch my back. Said karma would get me. Stuff like that. It pretty much continued for most of the reunion."

"Most but not all?" Julia asked. "Did he relent?"

"Right after he landed on his backside in the middle of the dance floor," Seth said. "He tried to cut in on our dance. He told Amy she could do better than me. Well, that's probably true—I don't deserve a wonderful woman like Amy—but you don't tell a girl that in front of the guy you're dissing."

"So you hit him?"

"Not exactly," he said. "When my doctor told me I'd ruin my knees unless I found a more gentle sport than parkour, I took up martial arts."

"Parkour?" Julia asked.

"Jumping off buildings and stuff," Seth said as if it was the most natural thing in the world to do. "Anyway, some of those martial arts moves are instinct. When Amy and I ignored him and went back to dancing, he put his hand on my shoulder. I guess he thought he was going to start something. I kind of went into ninja mode and he landed on the floor. Amy was impressed, and Dan never bothered me after that."

"But it's likely he was still angry."

"Probably more angry than when he got there," Seth said. "I mean, I dropped him hard. Not that I would have done that if I had thought about it. I'm not proud of it."

"Do you know how to reach Dan, what he does for a living, or anything else that would help me find him?"

"Kenton probably does," Seth said. "We got a roster from the reunion. I'll ask him to pull up a copy from my emails and send it to you. As to what he does, last I heard he was driving a truck."

"Thank you." Julia paused. "You're giving Kenton a lot to do. I can't help but notice you're not writing any of this down. Are you sure you'll remember all of it?"

Seth pointed to his head. "It's all up here. I don't write things down. It just clutters up the place."

"I'm the opposite. If I don't write it down, I'm likely to forget." She looked down at her notebook. "Tell me about Kenton."

His eyes narrowed. "You don't think he had something to do with Bosco's disappearance, do you?"

Julia sat back in her chair, subtly mirroring his position. "Do you?"

"No way," he said firmly. "Kenton Hollis is my business partner. I've known him since seventh grade. He's been my best friend since eighth grade."

"It took a year?" she asked in a teasing tone to lighten the mood.

"Well, there was this girl in our advanced English class. We both had a thing for her, so there was a year when we weren't exactly buddies. Then she dumped both of us on the same day to go to the homecoming dance with another guy. I guess we kind of bonded over our shared heartache."

Julia laughed. "What happened to the girl?"

"She moved that summer and we never heard from her again, so no point in putting her on the list. Speaking of the list, I feel bad about mentioning that restaurant lady. What's her name? Sooz?"

"Yes, Sooz Winter."

"Yeah, Amy's place took a lot of her lunch customers. I know she didn't like that. Who would? I'm a businessman. I get it. But the thing is, whoever took Bosco seemed to know that Amy kept him up in her apartment or was with him when he was out in the back garden. There wouldn't have been any time when he was alone and vulnerable to kidnapping from the house."

"So whoever wanted to take him had to know that."

"I think the kidnapping was arranged and not an accident. I doubt someone just saw that woman let go of the leash and then decided, 'Hey, I'll make some money off this.'" He crumpled up the taco wrapper. "He's out there somewhere, and Amy's heart is breaking. I just want Bosco back."

When Seth looked at Julia again, his expression was grim. "You have to get him back. I cannot express to you how important it is to have him returned."

"I think you just did," she said. "Let's go back to this Julia Child card for a minute. Who facilitated that sale?"

"You mean did I buy through a broker?" At her nod, he continued. "No, I bought the card in an open sale at a reputable auction house. The name is in the pleadings. You'll recognize it."

"I did," Julia said. "So with no go-between, the only parties to the sale were you, the estate that was selling the card, and the auction house."

"Correct. They did all the work of authenticating the piece and making sure the sale was legal. Actually, their lawyers were the ones who alerted us to the possible suit."

"Did they think it had merit?"

He shrugged. "I was told they just wanted us to know. Merit didn't come up in the conversation."

Julia placed her pen next to her notebook and rested her hands in her lap. "Thank you for your help. Meredith and I will interview everyone on this list. If you think of anything else that you believe will help us find this person, please contact me."

"Absolutely. In the meantime, would it help if I sent some folks out to look for Bosco in the neighborhoods around Forsyth Park?"

"That would be great," she said. "At this point we won't turn down any help. I've spoken to some of the regulars there and no one saw him, but there's so much going on down there in the late afternoon and evening, it isn't surprising that someone wouldn't notice a little dog running around."

"I'll make it happen." He paused. "Who am I kidding? Kenton will make it happen. I'll let you know if we find him."

Seth changed the subject, talking first about his love for food truck tacos and then jovially complaining of his futile effort to convince Amy to sell them in her restaurant. "'Not even on Tuesdays' is always her response." He paused, his face suddenly solemn. "I love her so much, Julia. I still cannot believe she's mine. I mean, let's face it. I'm a nerdy guy who preferred reading to just about anything else in high school."

"Amy is a wonderful woman," she agreed.

"She'll be great on television," he said. "I've got media lined up to try to get some movement on this case. Not that I don't think you ladies are worth what I'm paying you, but there's nothing wrong with getting the word out. My PR team is the best."

"I'm glad to have the help." She gathered up her pen and notebook and tucked them into her purse. "In the meantime, we'll keep looking."

Julia rose, and Seth scrambled to stand. His gaze met hers. "I'm trying to act cool here, but I'm not going to lie. I'm desperate to get that dog back. Today isn't soon enough. I would do anything. Anything," he said, his voice rising.

"I understand."

But as Julia left, she wondered if she did. She also wondered if there was something Seth wasn't telling her.

Chapter Seven

Savannah, Georgia
March 13, 1905

SALE SUCCESSFUL STOP OB HEALTHY AND WHOLE.

This news reached Cora by telegram within the hour, just as she was putting Monday lunch on the table at the boardinghouse on Oglethorpe Street. She could have returned to Savannah years ago as a wealthy woman and enjoyed a comfortable life.

Instead, Cora took rooms around the corner from the boardinghouse where she and Mama had once lived. She returned to the choir at the Methodist church where she sang soprano every Sunday morning. A year after she arrived, the rooming house on Oglethorpe Street became available, and Cora quietly purchased it and moved in as cook, cleaning crew, and landlady along with Ida, a former employee of her parents.

And she'd never been happier. Between running the boardinghouse and singing in the choir, her life was full. She still missed Mama and Mr. Price, but she was content and her days were full.

Cora's one concession to a previous life was to keep tabs on Oscar Bryant. Not directly, of course, but through a carefully chosen private detective agency, the Wilbert Trask Detective Agency. Mr. Trask preferred to correspond by telegram.

Originally Cora thought she might want to return to Oscar's kitchen and bake a cake with him, perhaps on her next birthday. Then the date for her departure came around, and she couldn't manage to leave Savannah. The same thing happened in 1904. Then this year.

All three years she purchased a ticket only to tuck it unused into the box in the attic.

The detective agency continued to send telegrams and draw their pay, and Cora continued to keep every one of those telegrams in a carefully hidden box in the attic. Then came the day when word arrived that Oscar was in trouble. He'd run afoul of men who demanded payments Oscar wasn't willing to make. His restaurant and his life were in danger.

Cora saw that the payment was made, though Mr. Trask advised against it.

"Pay these guys once and they know they've got you. They'll never leave you alone."

"But you'll figure out how to make that happen, won't you?" was her response.

And he had. For a year there was no further trouble from the thugs. Then came what Mr. Trask called a change of leadership. With that change came a man known as Bennie the Butcher.

And Bennie the Butcher wanted Oscar's place, or he wanted Oscar on his team. Unfortunately Oscar refused to cooperate with either option.

Having learned of the situation, which once again might have cost the stubborn man his life, Cora instructed Mr. Trask to broker a deal that would see Oscar's restaurant quietly sold to someone other than Bennie the Butcher. Then that buyer—Cora—would hand the keys over to Bennie. The deal was done, and Oscar was not only still alive but none the wiser.

Cora's only regret was that she could no longer return to the kitchen where she'd made one of her fondest memories. But at least the man she had made that memory with would remain alive.

She tucked the telegram into her apron pocket. Later, after she washed the lunch dishes, Cora would make the climb into the attic to add this telegram to the others. For now there was work to be done.

***

With the money safely deposited in his bank, he was free to do what he wanted.

Now in his thirties, Oscar was old enough to recognize this swift windfall as a blessing that might not ever come around again, and yet he was still young enough to consider doing something completely irresponsible with the profits. Something that didn't involve running a restaurant, even though that was all he had done for the past few years of his life. That *and dodge Bennie the Butcher and his men, but that was another story. The thugs had mysteriously elected to leave him alone despite the fact that he'd stood up to them, first when they demanded a welcome-to-the-neighborhood payment and then when they came around looking for him to sell out.*

Eventually Oscar had sold out, not to Bennie, though as he thought of it now, the company who purchased it could have been a front for the notorious thug.

Either way, Oscar was surprised that he felt pretty good about it. Even if Bennie ended up with the place, that was fine by him.

Before he chose his next path, Oscar had some unfinished business to handle. Twice in his life, he had made choices that he later wished he had not.

All the money in the world would not allow him to repair the damage he'd done when he snuck out of Atlanta, Georgia, with the life savings of the piano maker who had taken him in when no one else would. The old man was likely dead by now, but surely there were relatives to whom Oscar could make amends.

He opened the door of the Wilbert Trask Detective Agency without hesitation and stepped into a well-appointed lobby, where a secretary took his name and appointment time. A few minutes later, Oscar was led into a conference room, where a nondescript man in an ill-fitting dark suit was waiting.

The detective looked timid at best and downright forget-table too as he wrote something on the pad in front of him, then looked up at Oscar. "Not what you were expecting?" The fellow motioned for Oscar to take a seat across from him.

Oscar took in the man's slight build and pale complexion as he settled onto the chair. "I'll admit I am surprised. Are you Wilbert Trask?"

"That's me, and let me just say right off that the way I look is not accidental, Mr. Bryant."

Oscar noticed the quality of the pen in his hand and the diamond stickpin in his tie. Apparently detective work paid well.

"People look right past me thinking I'm of no threat to them," Trask continued. "Generally they are exceptionally surprised when later they are informed of who I am."

"I can see that," Oscar said then thought better of his comment. "I'm sorry, that was unkind of me."

"It was honest," Trask said. "And I prefer an honest client any day of the week. So how can I help you?"

"I need to find a man, or if he's dead, his next of kin," Oscar said. "And I need you to be discreet about it."

"What was his last known address, do you know?"

Oscar gave Trask the location of the piano maker's building in Atlanta. "Like I said, it's possible he's not still alive. It's been a long time since I saw him last."

"How long?"

Thirty years, seven months, and eighteen days, Oscar could have said, for he would never forget the date he'd made that choice. "Approximately thirty years," was the answer he gave.

Trask nodded and wrote on his pad again. "You want to meet the guy, or just be told where he is?" he asked, continuing to take notes.

"If he's alive, I want to meet him."

The detective looked up. "Okay, I'll arrange that. And if he's dead?"

"Then I want to know if he had a will, and if so, I will need a list of his next of kin. I don't want to meet them, but I will need to send them something important, so I'll need to know where they live."

Trask nodded. "Anything else I should know?"

Again Oscar gave the question a moment's thought. He could have informed Trask that there were likely theft charges still pending against him in the state of Georgia but kept that to himself. Returning the money came first, for if he turned himself in there would be little opportunity to do right by a family he'd done so very wrong.

Oscar shook his head.

"You've been told the fee?"

"I have," he said. "And I've brought a bank draft to pay half. The remainder will be delivered to you when you've completed the assignment. Those are the terms as I understand them."

"Yeah, that's it." Trask put his pen down and sat back. "Okay, I've got a guy down in Atlanta. I'll get him on this."

"Excellent. Thank you, Mr. Trask." He hesitated a moment. "There's something else."

Trask's brows rose. "Okay."

"I need you to find someone else for me." Oscar paused. *"Someone who disappeared on January 19, 1902."*

He let out a long breath and picked up his pen. "That's a specific date, so I figure there's a story that goes with it, or you wouldn't remember it so exactly."

"There is," he said, "but I don't need to tell it. You know almost everything about her that I do."

"Now you've got my attention. Who is she?"

"Coraline."

"Last name?" Trask asked without looking up from his writing.

"Just Coraline."

Understanding dawned on the detective's face. "The opera singer?"

Oscar nodded. "She's the one."

Trask dropped his pen. "What are you, some reporter? Nobody knows where that lady went. She walked out of her hotel room two days after a couple of concerts at Carnegie Hall and never looked back. As I understand it, she didn't even bother to take her belongings with her. Just dropped the key at the desk and left."

"Yes, that's the story I heard too."

"So you don't know a different one?"

Oscar shook his head. "No, I don't."

Trask studied him a minute then frowned. "So you wanna hire me to find this singer, and you've got no information other than what I can read in the papers. And you think I've got the chops to find her."

A statement, not a question.

"*I do.*"

"*She could be anywhere. No one knows anything about her. The guy who was managing her career died two weeks before she did her big exit.*"

"*I didn't know,*" Oscar said.

"*Yeah, he was on that train that crashed in the Park Avenue tunnel. Awful mess. I had a buddy injured in that accident. It's a miracle anyone walked away.*" Trask stopped speaking and appeared to be thinking. Then he shrugged. "*Give me one clue about her that I wouldn't know and maybe I'll take this.*"

He thought. Had she said anything during their evening together that had given something of her past away? Her mother baked cakes. She added cardamom to them.

Oscar frowned as frustration welled up. Coraline had said very little.

Then it hit him.

"*You've got something,*" Trask said. "*I can see it on your face.*"

"*I do,*" he told the detective. "*She's Southern.*"

"*How do you know that?*"

Rather than give up a single detail of the evening he held close to his heart, Oscar shrugged. "*Because I know, all right?*"

Oscar stuck out his hand to seal the deal. "*Just find her, Mr. Trask. I don't care how long it takes. I have to see her again.*"

The detective rested both palms on the table and regarded Oscar with a serious look. "That answers the first question. I've just got one more."

"Go ahead," Oscar said.

"What do you plan to do when you find her? I won't be part of something nefarious." His eyes narrowed and for the first time since the meeting began, Oscar saw the potential for violence in this seemingly meek man.

"Bake her a cake," he said.

Chapter Eight

JULIA'S PHONE RANG JUST AS she climbed into her car and started the engine. Cold air blew from the air conditioner vents, chasing the August heat that had already crept into the car's interior since she arrived for her meeting.

When she saw that the caller was Meredith, Julia put her on speaker as she answered. "Meredith, are you at the office yet?"

"Just got here. Apparently I had a nail in my tire. Chase was able to get it taken care of. Have I mentioned how much I'm enjoying having him home for a few days? Anyway, how did it go with Seth?"

Julia caught her up on what transpired during the interview. "I keep thinking over what Seth said about following the money and about access to the dog. If he's right about Amy's habits regarding Bosco, then the only way to grab the dog was to catch him away from home and away from Amy."

"So whoever took the dog knew he would be with a dog walker that day," Meredith said. "Everything goes back to Stephanie Sterling. She let go of the leash."

"That's the story anyway," Julia said. "I would like to hear her version of what happened."

"We need to talk to her," Meredith said. "And maybe the owner of the company who assigned her to the job."

"Agreed. Once we get both of their stories, we can compare notes. They may tell the same story, but they may not." Julia paused. "Can you believe after working so hard to get a reputation for solving difficult cases, we're looking for a lost dog?"

"Well, we've got our work cut out for us even if it is just a missing dog. So I guess our next step is to see if we can track down our dog walker and her boss and get more than just a description of the event from them. If Stephanie is being paid off by someone, then maybe we can coax that information out of her."

"And I want to have Carmen do a background check on Phil Weber. Seth said he offered the man a lot of money to keep the lawsuit from happening, but the guy wouldn't accept. That makes me wonder why."

Someone tapped on the car window, and Julia gasped. She looked up into the brown eyes of a tall man with mahogany skin and broad shoulders. He appeared to be about thirty or so, dressed in jeans and a red polo shirt with a Harvard logo.

He smiled and held up a business card with the name Kenton Hollis on it. She matched his grin.

"What's wrong?" Meredith asked. "What's happening?"

"Sorry," she said. "It looks like I'm about to talk to Kenton Hollis. He's Seth's friend and business partner. I'll call you when we're done."

Julia hung up and turned off the car. Then she retrieved her keys and opened the door.

"Julia Foley, right?" he asked when she stood and closed the car door behind her.

"Yes, that's right." She shook his hand when he offered it. "I'm glad you stopped me. I was actually going to try to track you down today to see if we could meet."

"I thought you might."

He handed her his business card. She noticed the address of the building she'd just left beneath his name but no corporate affiliation. Below the address was a series of ways to contact him from phone to email and several social media links.

"Go ahead and keep that in case you have any follow-up questions after we're done."

"Thank you." She tucked the card into her purse. "Did Seth send you out to find me?"

"No, I haven't been up yet. I saw on Seth's calendar that you were meeting with him, so I did my research on your company. Impressive."

"I'm very glad you think so," she said. "Meredith and I are proud of Magnolia Investigations."

"As well you should be." He paused. "Once you spoke to Seth, I figured the next logical step would be to find the man who could give you the names of people who might want to harm him."

"That's right," she said. "Seth mentioned you would have information for me."

"I'll see that it's sent to you."

Julia reached into her purse and handed him her card. "Email works best, though you can always fax it. I prefer not to have to read on my phone—old eyes and all—so texting isn't my favorite way of receiving a document. Would you have a few minutes for some questions now? I'd be happy to come back up to your office."

Kenton pocketed the card without looking at it. Then he glanced up at the building, presumably to the top floor where his boss might be watching them. "If you don't mind, could we take a walk?"

"Of course." She clicked the LOCK button on her car and tucked her keys in her purse. Together they set out toward Johnson Square. The oldest and largest of the squares in Savannah, the parklike square was one of Julia's favorites. Unlike the busy Forsyth Park just steps from the office, this one was quiet and offered spaces for contemplation and reflection.

They walked for a few minutes in silence, crossing the intersection of Congress and Bull Streets to step into the park just as the bell at Christ Church Episcopal—crafted by Revere & Son in 1819— tolled the hour. She remembered that detail—that the family of Paul Revere was responsible for the bell—from one of the many stories of Savannah that her mama told her as a child.

"Is it ten o'clock already?" Julia asked, checking her watch.

"I'm guessing Seth plied you with tacos and stories of how much he loves Amy in addition to answering your questions. He usually does."

The tone Kenton used when speaking of Amy caught her attention. Julia tried to make light of it while trying to discover why. She gave him a sideways look. "Don't like tacos?"

His chuckle was a low rumbling sound that made Julia smile. "Okay, you got me there. Yes, I love tacos and so does Seth. That's why he runs on Tuesday mornings. He figures if he does his run he can eat all the tacos he wants afterward."

"Not a bad way to look at life." She paused then decided to surprise Kenton with the question that was uppermost on her mind. "You don't like Amy much, do you?"

He glanced around then nodded to a bench in the shade. "How about we sit a while?"

Julia settled beside him on the bench. With its view of one of the park's two fountains and the white marble obelisk dedicated to Nathaniel Green, it was easy to forget that the traffic of Savannah hurried past just beyond.

Until a horn honked, drowning out the splash of the fountain.

She reached into her purse for her pen and notebook. "I believe we were talking about whether you liked Amy or not."

"My feelings toward Amy are not relevant," he said. "What is relevant is anything that will get that dog back."

"Okay," Julia said. "That may be, but I'm investigating who might have a reason to take Bosco. I have to include anyone who doesn't like her as someone who might benefit from her distress."

His back straightened. "So you're thinking I might have something to do with the theft." Another chuckle. "Lady, if I could tell you what I know..."

"You can." She left those two words hanging between them. Then she added, "I presume you wanted to speak here instead of up there in your office so Seth wouldn't hear what you might say. Am I wrong?"

"You are not," he said with a sigh. "Though if you think I had anything to do with that dog's disappearance, you're mistaken."

"Then tell me why, please." She was silent a moment. "Look, I'm a former judge. You know that since you've researched the company. I tend to be plainspoken, but I'm not accusing you of anything. I would like to rule you out, and I would also like to hear whatever you know that might help Meredith and me do our jobs."

He nodded and then said nothing further for a moment. "Okay, the topic of Amy is a sore subject," he finally said. "She's smart and funny and is a great cook, obviously. She makes cinnamon rolls better than anyone I know."

"I had them yesterday," Julia said with a smile. "They are delicious."

Kenton leaned forward to rest his elbows on his knees. "So when you ask if I like her, sure, I like her just fine."

"You just don't like her with Seth," she offered.

"You've got that backward," he said. "I don't like Seth with her."

Her gaze fell to his left hand, where she noticed he wore no wedding ring. Then she looked back up at Kenton, who was studying something off in the distance.

"Tell me why you feel this way."

"Seth probably told you that he and I have been friends since we were kids. We were an unlikely pair, him a skinny white boy and me an African American kid who wanted nothing more than to play pro baseball like my dad. But we had one thing in common other than the fact we sat beside each other in homeroom. We were smart. And it wasn't cool to be smart."

Dappled sunlight shifted as a warm breeze blew past. Julia let the comment settle between them and said nothing.

He pressed his palms onto his knees. "Anyway, we both survived, and here we are." Kenton looked at her. "It turned out pretty great for both of us. We're partners in a business that we never thought would get off the ground."

"And now you're doing quite well."

"Probably better than Seth realizes. He's not much into the financial side of things. If he can buy his tacos and running gear, he's pretty happy. Or was."

"Why do you say that?"

"Amy takes his mind off his work. Sure, he likes being with her, but he's also stressing over attending meetings and he's delegating things he used to handle himself. Which is why I'm not keen on the two of them as a couple."

"Kenton," Julia said. "Are you jealous of Amy's friendship with him?"

Chapter Nine

KENTON SAT BACK ABRUPTLY. "WHAT? No. Nothing like that." He exhaled. "Seth has lost his focus. He'd rather be with Amy than work on the business. Now that this dog is missing, he's impossible. Then there's the expense."

"What do you mean?" Julia asked.

"Seth spends a lot of money on that woman," Kenton grumbled.

"Company money?"

"His, but that doesn't mean it doesn't worry me. You have no idea what he's lost if that dog isn't found."

"Go on," she said.

Kenton shook his head. "I've said too much."

He rose. Julia stood, tucking her notebook and pen into her bag.

"I'll get you my list of anyone who's given us or the company grief," he said.

"You already have one?" Julia asked.

"Yeah." Kenton met her gaze. "Part of what I do is look after the business, and looking after the business sometimes means looking after Seth. I've been doing that since high school when Dan Bell decided Seth was his personal punching bag."

Interesting. Seth had also mentioned Bell.

"Have you kept up with him?"

"I know where he is and have a vague idea of what he's up to, but that's about it."

"Are you friends with him?"

"No way." He shrugged. "I check out the high school alumni page occasionally. Unless things have changed, he drives a truck and lives in his grandparents' house. And yes, he's on the list I'll be sending you. I don't know if Seth told you about our recent high school reunion."

Kenton smiled as they set off walking. "I was so proud of him for dropping that guy. It was about fifteen years too late, but Seth didn't have his ninja skills back then."

"Dan couldn't have been happy about being embarrassed like that," Julia said.

"Probably not." He shrugged again. "But to abduct a poodle over it?"

"Bosco is a miniature schnauzer."

"Right. Well, anyway, yeah, he was mad. So maybe."

"This is going to seem like a random question, but do you happen to know either the dog walker who lost Bosco or the owner of the company that hired her? Amy made a comment that the company came highly recommended. Did you recommend them?"

Kenton frowned. "Yes. Seth comes to me all the time with requests like that. I'm pretty connected to local businesses—I have to be, given what I do—so I asked around and found them."

They emerged from the park, pausing at the intersection until the light changed and the signal appeared for them to walk across. Heat was rising from the pavement, giving a hint at the warmth of the afternoon to come.

Once they reached the other side, Julia decided to ask one more question. "Kenton, where do you think Bosco is?"

He stopped short and looked down at Julia. "If I knew, we wouldn't be having this conversation."

"Okay, that's fair." They continued walking until they reached her car. "Just one more thing. If you were me, who would you be talking to next?"

"My guess is you've already talked to her."

Julia shook her head. "And who is that?"

"Amy."

She decided not to tell him she already had. "Why?"

"I'm a numbers guy," he said. "And a businessman. I don't like to brag, but I learned from the best at Harvard, and I think I'm pretty good at what I do. I also own a number of small businesses under my corporate umbrella. I know what I'm talking about. Follow the money. The only person I see profiting from this whole thing is Amy Bryant."

"You're going to have to explain that," Julia said. "Because right now Amy is the only person who seems to be truly hurting over this. I know Seth is upset, but Amy can barely stop crying over Bosco."

Julia had said the words a bit more vehemently that she'd intended. She tried again. "I'm sorry. I don't think you were finished with what you were going to say."

Kenton shook his head. "No, it's fine. Amy is a likable woman. I've already told you all the reasons I like her. But if you follow the money, you'll see that she's getting a whole bunch of free publicity right now courtesy of Seth and our PR department. Her posters are all over. Sales are up—I know this because I also do her accounting—and people can't get enough of the human interest side of this story."

"Seth mentioned he'd be getting the word out."

"His name opens a lot of doors in this town. Bottom line is, you watch," Kenton said. "That dog will show up soon enough. In the meantime Amy will milk it for all it's worth. And it's worth a whole lot of new customers."

"Are you saying you think that Bosco isn't lost at all and that Amy has created a fake crisis in order to raise her sales?"

"Increased sales are a great incentive, I'm guessing." Kenton glanced down at his watch.

Julia remained silent a moment. Although the scenario Kenton proposed went against everything she thought true about Amy, in theory it had merit.

"You made a statement earlier that if you could tell me what you knew…" She gave Kenton a direct look. "What do you know that you haven't told me?"

His expression went from surprise to a slow grin. "You are every bit as good of an investigator as the reports say you are. Unfortunately, I'm out of time. Have a good rest of your day, Julia."

Kenton turned to walk toward the entrance to the Manger Building. "Kenton," she called. "Can I ask just one more question?"

He stopped short and turned around. After what appeared to be a moment of hesitation, he walked back to Julia. "Sure."

"You said that Seth is putting money and his PR folks behind the search. Is his company profiting from Amy's increased sales?"

At first she didn't think he would answer. Then he shook his head. "There are financial agreements, yes, but I'm not at liberty to say anything beyond that."

"Why?"

"You were a judge, Mrs. Foley. You know that some things are not to be shared, no matter what."

No matter what. The connotation of that statement weighed on her.

Kenton Hollis seemed to be a man whose interest was in protecting his friend and their business. But how far would he go to do those things?

"Thank you for your time," she told him. "And your help."

His smile was quick and broad. Then he waved and walked away.

Chapter Ten

Savannah, Georgia
March 18, 1905

Cora was peeling potatoes for the Saturday evening meal when she spied the messenger boy dropping his bicycle on the sidewalk outside. She wiped her hands on the dish towel she'd slung over her shoulder and took a few coins from the jar in the back of the pie safe.

After pausing to retrieve an oatmeal cookie and tuck it into the pocket of her apron, Cora walked to the door to greet the lad.

Timmy was the spitting image of his father, with whom she'd grown up, a reminder of how familiar things were here in Savannah. Likely Mama would have offered Timmy's father a cookie and some coins just as Cora was doing now. This reminder and its connection to Mama were two more reasons why Cora was very glad to be home, even after all these years.

"A message for one of my boarders, Timmy?"

He offered a broad grin. "It's for you this time, Miss St. Germaine."

Her smile faltered. "Well now, thank you. Would you mind waiting a moment to see if I have a response?"

Time was of the essence for messenger boys. The more deliveries they made, the better they were paid. This was why she sweetened her offer, both literally and figuratively.

"Here are a few coins for your trouble." While he was tucking the money into the pocket of his trousers, Cora retrieved the cookie. "And something to chew on while I go in and read the telegram."

"Thank you," he said, his eyes sparkling. "I do love your oatmeal cookies. I'll just wait right here, then."

She walked back inside, each step twisting her thoughts toward a fear she tried not to allow. Cora closed the door behind her and leaned against it, steadying herself as she opened the telegram with shaking hands.

It was from Mr. Trask.

He wants me to find you. Yes or no?

Cora let out the breath she didn't realize she'd been holding. For a moment, the room threatened to spin. Then she squared her shoulders and walked into the kitchen to find the pencil and paper she'd been using to make a grocery list. After tearing off a sheet, she wrote one word and folded it then walked outside to hand it to Timmy along with two more cookies.

"Please have this sent as a response to the telegram you just delivered. And say hello to your family for me."

Timmy grinned as he tucked the note and one of the two cookies into his pocket. He rode away with one hand on his handlebars and the other holding a cookie to his mouth.

"Be careful, Timmy," she called. "Both hands on your handlebars, please."

He waved in response and then turned to disappear down Abercorn Street. How long Cora stood there, her heart racing and her fists clenched, she couldn't say.

Finally, she walked back into the boardinghouse. Rather than return to the kitchen and her duties there, she made the trek up to the attic, where she tossed the telegram into the box with the others.

The one word she'd sent in reply chased her back down the stairs along with her fears and no small measure of regret. It was for the best.

"No," she whispered as she went back to peeling potatoes. "I had to say no, Oscar. There just wasn't any other answer."

Chapter Eleven

As soon as Kenton disappeared into the building, Julia climbed into her car. After turning the key in the ignition and ensuring that the air conditioner vents were blowing full strength on her, she dialed Meredith's number.

"I'm headed back to the office after I cool off," she said.

"Was the AC broken?"

Julia chuckled. "No, Kenton wanted to take a walk, so I interviewed him while sitting on a bench in Johnson Square."

"Okay," Meredith said in a surprised tone. "Was that your choice or his?"

"His. I'll tell you everything we talked about when I get there."

Julia looked at the clock on her dashboard. "I can be there by eleven. Want to just come out and jump into the car? How about we have lunch at the Downhome Diner when we're done?"

"Sounds great. I'll be watching for you," she said.

Ten minutes later, Meredith stepped out the back door of the office with two travel mugs bearing the Magnolia Investigations logo, one of which she presented to Julia. "Diet Dr Pepper. I figured you'd want some after Taco Tuesday and your walk in the park."

Meredith placed her purse on the floor of the car then climbed inside. She placed her cup in the holder and buckled her seat belt.

Julia laughed. "Thank you. If we keep being fed at every interview, I'm going to have to take up running again."

"It is August, Jules," Meredith said. "You can jog in this heat if you want, but if you see me running it's because someone is chasing me or there's a half-price sale at the designer outlet. Now before we go anywhere tell me what you've learned so far."

Julia gave Meredith a quick summary of her conversation with Kenton. "So what do you think of all that?"

"I think he knows more than he's saying." Meredith reached down to retrieve a notepad from her purse. "While I was waiting for you, I did a little research on Woof Walk."

"Did you find the name of the owner?"

"It's owned by a corporation based in Delaware. I'm still trying to track down who owns the corporation and whether there's a local angle to this. It could be some big company with no connection to Savannah at all. I'll find out. Anyway, the manager's name is Brian Duffy."

"Did you call to let Brian Duffy know we're coming?"

She affected an innocent look. "I probably should have. It would be the polite thing to do rather than just barge in unannounced." Then she grinned. "But I thought about it and decided it might be best to catch him there without expecting us."

"I agree."

Meredith's phone rang. She glanced down at the screen then back up at Julia. "It's Chase. Give me just a sec."

"Of course." Julia picked up her phone and began scrolling through her emails.

"Chase, sweetheart. What's up?"

Julia was engrossed in reading when Meredith hung up. Julia glanced up at her. "Everything okay?"

"Chase called from the office. He dropped by to surprise me and take me to lunch." She paused. "Do you mind terribly if I let him? We can go to Woof Walk when I get back."

Julia reached to turn the car off. "I don't mind a bit. My morning interviews have given me plenty of things to research. Why don't we plan on doing this tomorrow?" She thought for a moment. "Just in case you want to spend the afternoon with your son."

Meredith grinned. "Perfect."

***

The next morning, Julia and Meredith pulled into a parking space at the far end of a 1980s era tan metal shopping center situated south of the city. After checking the directory, they found the office of Woof Walk tucked into a corner between a nail salon and a janitorial supply store.

A bell on the door jangled as Meredith stepped inside first with Julia right behind her. The space that passed for a reception area was dingy and dimly lit with paneled walls and stained orange carpet. Two chairs upholstered in a plaid that may have matched the carpet at one time flanked a floor lamp with a crooked shade and a burned-out light bulb.

A narrow hallway led around to what appeared to be several doors that might be offices. At the end of the hall an upright vacuum cleaner older than the one Julia's mother still used sat next to a bucket with a mop poised inside.

"Hello?" Meredith called. "Mr. Duffy, are you here?"

The hum of an air conditioner somewhere in the back of the office and a radio turned to a sports talk show were the only sounds. Julia and Meredith exchanged glances. Then Meredith tried again.

"Anyone here?"

No response.

She reached into her purse to retrieve her phone and notebook then dialed. A moment later, a phone rang somewhere in the distance. Then it rang again.

After a third ring, it stopped. Julia looked over at Meredith, who was smiling.

"Yes, hello. This is Meredith Bellefontaine. No, actually I didn't call to talk about walking a dog." She met Julia's gaze and grinned. "I can explain, but you're going to have to come to the lobby." A pause. "Yes, Mr. Duffy. The lobby of your office."

The sound of the radio disappeared. Then a door opened and a bearded man who looked to be in his late forties appeared in the hallway.

Wearing khaki cargo shorts, a blue fishing shirt, and sandals, he walked toward them. "Mrs. Bellefontaine?"

Meredith put her phone away. "Yes, please call me Meredith, and this is Julia." She produced a business card and held it out to him. "And you must be Brian Duffy."

"Call me Duff," he said, accepting the business card from Meredith.

"Julia and I own Magnolia Investigations," Meredith said. "We're here to talk about—"

"She doesn't work here anymore."

"Stephanie Sterling," Meredith finished.

"Like I said, she doesn't work here anymore." He shrugged. "Steph was a nice kid, but we can't keep anyone on the payroll who loses dogs. It's not like my employees to put our dogs in danger."

"No, but you did put Bosco in danger," Meredith said. "And he's still missing."

"Yeah, I know." He tugged at his beard. "I get this daily email update from corporate, and they like to remind me of that."

"Who sends those emails?" Meredith asked.

He shrugged. "No clue. Just someone from corporate."

"Do you know Amy Bryant or Seth Stevenson?" Meredith continued.

Duff looked as if he was considering how to answer.

"It's a yes or no question," Julia said.

"I know who they are," Duff said. "Who wouldn't? Much as it's a big city, Savannah is still a small town. If you listen to the radio or watch television news, then you've heard Amy Bryant talking about how much she misses her dog. I actually cried when I heard her talking about the little guy."

Julia gave Meredith a sideways look. "Where is Stephanie Sterling now?"

"Don't have any idea," he said. "I have a phone number that she gave me when she filled out the employment forms. I probably shouldn't pass it on, but if it'll help you find that dog, I'd be glad to give it to you."

"Thank you," Meredith said. "That would be helpful."

"Come on back here to my office, and I'll get it." He led them down the corridor to the second door on the right. When he stepped inside, Julia and Meredith followed.

Duff's office stood in stark contrast to the shabby waiting area up front. A leather sofa was positioned on one wall beneath a collection of Savannah Banana baseball team memorabilia.

"I've had season tickets since the Bananas' opening season," Duff said as he sat behind his desk and opened a drawer. "My kids love it. Woof Walk always sponsors a dog in the pup race. That bowl of bananas over there on the bookshelf is the trophy we won back in 2017."

"Beau and I have been to a few games," Julia said. "It's a lot of fun."

Duff nodded but didn't look up from his search. Then he pulled out a folder and placed it on his desk. "Here it is. Now I can't let you look at this, but I can give you a phone number."

As Duff recited the number, Meredith wrote it down. "Thank you," she said. "Now if you've got a minute, Julia and I would like to ask you a couple of questions."

Duff looked hesitant but he finally nodded and gestured to the chairs across the desk from him. "Like I told you before, I don't know anything. Just that the dog was lost and I fired the girl. That's all I can tell you."

"Be that as it may," Meredith began, "I think you may be able to help. Is—was—Stephanie your only employee?"

"No, we have a couple of regulars who have been with Woof Walk for years. Marvis is a librarian, but she works flexible hours, so we use her several times a week for small groups. Now Farris, he's been here the longest. He works afternoons only—he's a night owl— and has been retired as long as I've known him. He's got season tickets next to me at the Bananas games, so I see him more at the games than here. I'm usually gone for the day when he gets here around four. Compared to the year and a half we had Stephanie, the other two are pros."

"Would you please give us their phone numbers too?"

"Why? They wouldn't know anything about what happened to that dog. Neither of them were working when it happened," he protested.

"I understand," Meredith told him, "but they may have seen or heard something. Maybe a fellow pet owner said something that could be pertinent to this case. In our line of work we never know where the next clue will come from."

"I just don't feel right about doing that," he said.

"Okay," Meredith said. "Do you know a man named Kenton Hollis?"

Duff's expression went slack. "Why?"

"It might help," Julia said. "My guess is you do."

"I'd rather not talk about it." He stood. "I need to be somewhere soon, so I'm going to have to walk you out."

"How do you know him?" Meredith asked. "Because Julia just spoke to him a little while ago. He's got a lot of information he's going to be sending to her regarding people who might be potential suspects in this dognapping. Is your name going to be on that list?"

Duff's eyes widened. "I did not steal that dog," he said. "If you try to prove otherwise, I will have my lawyers on you so fast it'll make your head spin."

"Duff," Julia said evenly, "the only thing Meredith and I are trying to prove is the whereabouts of Amy Bryant's dog. If your name comes up in the investigation, we'll follow that lead. And if you're guilty of something, we'll find that out sooner or later."

"I'm not guilty of anything," Duff said.

An idea struck her. "Duff," Julia said, "do you think Kenton Hollis had anything to do with Amy's dog being taken?"

"Really, I gotta go." He hurried to the front door and opened it. "Sorry, you're going to have to leave."

They did as he asked and stepped out into the sweltering August heat. A moment later, Duff closed the door and locked it.

"Bingo," Meredith said. "There's a connection between Woof Walk and Seth Stevenson's best friend. That's no coincidence."

Julia clicked the button to unlock her car. Once inside, she blasted the air-conditioning and waited for Meredith to climb in.

"I have a feeling Kenton's name is going to come up when you finally get to the end of the rabbit trail of ownership on that corporation you've been researching."

"Yes, that's a possibility," Meredith said. "There's definitely a connection somewhere."

"Let's see what Stephanie Sterling has to say," Julia said. "Maybe she knows something."

"Considering the possibility that she let the leash go on purpose, I'd say she probably does know something. But will she admit to what she knows?" Meredith shrugged. "I'm not so sure she will."

After calling Stephanie but being sent straight to voice mail, Meredith was able to find an address for her online, and Julia drove to the address. It turned out to be a garage apartment behind a house just down the road from the Olde Pink House restaurant on Reynolds Square. As they walked up the narrow driveway, an older woman in a yellow sundress intercepted them.

"Are you looking to rent the apartment?"

Julia and Meredith exchanged glances. "This one?" Meredith asked. "I thought it was occupied."

"It was until little missy decided to pack her things and leave three nights ago. And she was already late on the rent."

"And she didn't leave a forwarding address?" Meredith asked.

The woman gave Meredith an incredulous look. "Does a person usually leave a forwarding address when they're skipping out on the rent? Of course she didn't."

"Would it be possible to take a look at the apartment?"

"Sure," she said. "Which are you, reporters or the law?"

"Neither." Meredith handed her a card. "We're investigating a lost dog."

"Of course. The famous lost dog. Who hasn't heard of it?" She tucked the card into her pocket and nodded toward the gate. "It isn't locked and neither is the apartment. I've got a cleaning service coming soon, so I made sure to open it for them. Go on up, but be prepared to get out of their way if they show up."

"Thank you," Meredith said. "We won't be long."

A thought occurred to Julia. "Do you know if any of her personal items are still there?"

"Didn't pay that much attention when I went up there. I saw the closet was empty, and that was enough for me. I figured she wouldn't empty it if she wasn't taking everything she wanted and not coming back. It's possible you'll find something of hers there. Like I said, the cleaners will haul off what isn't mine in a while, so look fast."

Meredith went first, negotiating the narrow wooden staircase up to the garage apartment with care. "This is a hazard," she told

Julia. "If I lived here, I'd probably break my neck just trying to go up and down these stairs."

The garage apartment was designed to mimic the stucco and wrought iron Spanish exterior of the main house. Where the style looked impressive on the mansion that sat facing the square, it looked more like a Las Vegas interpretation on the little apartment.

A black iron arrow motif decorated the door screen. Meredith pulled on the latch, and the screen gave way with a screech to reveal that one of the hinges was loose. The front door wore paint that had once been black. The wood was slightly warped but otherwise sturdy. It took some doing, but eventually Meredith got the latch to work and the door to open.

When Julia stepped inside, she immediately smelled the odor of mildew. The space appeared to be comprised of two rooms with wooden floors and white walls. The first room, a small living area with a kitchen at one end, had a blue and green plaid sofa, two tan overstuffed chairs, and a wooden cabinet.

One large window overlooked the street, the formerly white plastic blinds half-open and dingy. Julia turned to face the kitchen, the entirety of which was placed on one wall and punctuated by a tiny window.

The battered white refrigerator was minuscule and ancient, and the avocado-green stove wasn't much better. Someone had tried to bring some color to the space by painting the small amount of cabinetry lemon yellow. Meredith crossed the room, carefully stepping over a pile of laundry abandoned next to the sofa, and opened the refrigerator.

"Looks like she left some coffee creamer, a container of pimento cheese, and an empty carton of eggs." She straightened to survey the remainder of the space. "Nothing in the cabinets except a half-empty sleeve of saltine crackers. I can't tell if she's gone or just not very domesticated."

Julia moved into the bedroom, where, just as the landlady said, an empty closet answered the question. "She's gone."

Meredith stood in the doorway, one hand on her hip. "I see why she didn't take that bedding. It's frightful."

"Check the desk drawer," Julia said. "I'll dig around in the dresser and nightstand. See if she left anything that might help us."

Julia opened all three drawers on the dresser and found them empty. Then she went to the nightstand. An unopened bottle of water sat beside a stack of mystery novels and a Mason jar stuffed with wine corks. A poster tacked on the wall behind the nightstand advertised the local music festival held at the riverfront in 2017.

When she opened the top drawer, she found only a blank note-pad, a nearly full bottle of off-brand perfume, and a pink pen bearing a Sally's Ice Cream Shop logo. Julia closed the drawer and opened the bottom one.

It was empty.

"I think I've got something," Meredith called.

Julia hurried to join her and leaned down to peer at a paper among the debris that spilled out of the overflowing trash can. "Is that a deposit slip?"

Meredith looked up at her and nodded. "It sure is. The name on the account is Stephanie Sterling, and look at that amount."

"Whoa," Julia said softly. "No way she made five thousand dollars walking dogs."

Meredith retrieved her phone and snapped a picture then stood. "No, but how about for dropping a leash?"

Chapter Twelve

JULIA GLANCED AROUND STEPHANIE'S APARTMENT then returned her attention to Meredith. "I think we need to photograph all of this."

"Agreed." Meredith paused. "The person who paid Stephanie to drop that leash had a reason for it. We both know that. I just wish I knew what it was."

"Well, either the person wanted to capture Bosco alive or wanted the dog…" She didn't complete that sentence. It was the first time she'd considered that something might happen to the little dog.

"Wanted him dead," Meredith supplied. "I've thought of that option but didn't really want to say it out loud. We have to consider it though."

Julia nodded. "If someone really wanted to get even with Amy for something, that would definitely be a way to do it. I want to be wrong about that, though."

"So do I," Meredith said. "Either way we'll find out what happened to Bosco. I'll take these pictures, then I think we need to call the police, don't you?"

Julia thought a moment. "If we do that, they'll seal the apartment, and everything will likely be taken into evidence."

"That's a good thing, right?" Meredith asked. "It will preserve clues."

"Yes, but it's possible Stephanie will lawyer up, and then we won't be able to interview her." She looked over at Meredith. "She's the only person who saw Bosco escape."

"As far as we know," Meredith said.

"Yes, right." Julia paused. "We need to talk to her. She may know where Bosco is."

Meredith leaned against the empty dresser. "What about the little black dog that Beau saw running toward the park?"

"There are lots of little black dogs in Savannah. That one might not have been Bosco."

"Oh, Jules," Meredith said. "You've given me an idea. Let's go back to the possibility that someone may just be trying to take a jab at Amy. I think we also need to consider that Bosco might be sold. What do you think?"

She groaned. "I hadn't even considered it, but you're right. It's certainly possible."

Meredith punched in a number on her phone. A moment later she hit the SPEAKER button and the sound of Carmen answering filled the room.

"Carmen," Meredith said, "we've got an assignment for you. When Carl comes in with the mail today, I need you to ask him for contact information for his niece Stephanie Sterling. Preferably where she's living and working."

"Okay. He should be here in an hour or so. I'll make a note to ask him."

"Tell him I need to speak to him when he has time," Julia added. "If he could set an appointment, that would be great."

"Even if it's not during office hours?" Carmen asked.

"I'll make an exception in this case," Julia said.

"All right. Anything else?"

"Yes," Meredith said. "If my son shows up there, tell him he's taking Mama out for dinner tonight. The cupboards are bare, and I don't want to order pizza. We've got reservations for seven, but he'll have to call me back to find out where we're going. Oh, and since he bought lunch yesterday, I'll pay tonight."

Carmen laughed. "Okay. I don't expect him, but if he shows up, I'll pass that message on."

"Did he finish helping with the charity boxes?" Julia asked.

"We got them all done," she said. "Carl is picking them up this afternoon, so you'll have your conference room back. Thank you for allowing me to work in there."

"We weren't supposed to be here this week, so it's fine," Meredith said. "I'm glad Chase made himself useful."

"Oops, the other line is ringing," Carmen said.

"Go answer it," Meredith told her. "Remember we're supposed to be on vacation." She laughed.

"Will do. *Hasta la vista.*"

"Okay, that's handled." Meredith tucked her phone into her pocket. "Now what are we going to do about that deposit slip? Surely you don't think we should just leave it here? Anyone could come in here and take it."

"And the landlady said cleaners are coming, so either way it's going to be gone soon," Julia added. "But I don't feel comfortable just walking out of here with it if it could be evidence."

Meredith reached for her phone again. "I'm going to call Wally Parker. He'll know what to do."

Wally and Ron Bellefontaine, Meredith's late husband, had been on the police force together. Though Wally had already tried to retire down to the Florida Keys once, he'd gotten bored and returned to police work as a detective.

"Parker," came the gruff voice over the speaker.

"Wally, it's Meredith Bellefontaine." They exchanged pleasantries, and then she continued. "Do you have a minute to talk about something related to a case Julia and I are working on? It has to do with evidence in a suspected theft. We need some off-the-record advice."

"Anything for you ladies," he said. "Fire away."

Meredith gave Wally a summary of the case and how they ended up standing in Stephanie Sterling's apartment looking at a bank receipt for a deposit of five thousand dollars. "The landlady has cleaners coming to empty the apartment anytime. What do we do?"

"You say this woman whose dog was stolen reported the theft to the police?"

"She did," Julia said. "Amy told me an officer went out to talk to her and a few of the neighbors but ended up not making a report because he said it was likely the dog would come home."

"I can't say that I disagree," he said. "Just based on minimal facts, that is. But now you're telling me you've followed the trail and it has led to an apartment where you've found proof the dog walker made a big deposit shortly after the dog got away on her watch?"

"Yes, that's right," Meredith said. "The receipt says she deposited five thousand dollars."

"That's a lot of cash. Okay, let me think about this. How much is the dog worth?"

Meredith and Julia exchanged glances and then both shrugged. "I'll have Carmen check," Julia said. "The dog was an AKC registered animal, and I doubt they're inexpensive."

"How do you know that?" Meredith asked her.

She related the story of Amy writing a recipe on the dog's registration papers and handing it to Carmen in the grocery store on the day they first met. "I'm going to call Carmen and get a value for you, Wally. Give me just a minute."

While Wally and Meredith continued their conversation, Julia stepped into the living room and called Carmen.

"I'm good but not that good, Julia," Carmen said when she answered.

"I've actually got a question for you. I need to know how much an AKC registered miniature schnauzer is worth."

"Puppies start at around six hundred dollars, but depending on the bloodline, the price can be double that or more."

Julia was a bit taken aback. "You're sure?"

"Positive," Carmen told her. "When Amy got Bosco, I looked into getting one from that litter for me. They were so cute. But no *bueno* on the price. Maybe someday when my rich Prince Charming comes along, but not right now."

Julia laughed. "Are you actively seeking either?"

"Honestly I'd rather have the dog," she said. "But if the Lord sends a man to go with the puppy, I'm okay with that too."

"Thanks, Carmen," she said with a chuckle. Then she hung up and returned to the bedroom to share what Carmen had told her.

"Okay," Wally told them. "So not a million-dollar dog but also not a stray. Since the animal is arguably worth more than five hundred dollars, it is possible we're looking at a felony, though it's generally going to be considered a misdemeanor."

"But it's still a crime to take someone's dog, right?" Meredith insisted. "So what do we do about the potential evidence we've found when the officer doesn't want to take a report?"

"Off the record?"

"Of course," Julia said. "And I think I know what you're going to say."

"Photograph everything," he said.

"We did," Meredith told him.

"Find something to pick the receipt up with. Preserve any prints that might be on it. Put it in a zip-top bag if you've got one with you. If not, see that it's bagged as soon as you can."

"Then what?"

"Do the next thing you were planning to do," he said. "You did have a plan for after you searched the location, or am I wrong?"

"No, we do," Meredith said.

"Then do that. When you have more than circumstantial evidence regarding the dog, call me back. I would like to help you by opening a file on this, but since an officer has already looked into it and determined that a crime wasn't committed, I'm reluctant to step in without more to go on."

"We understand," Meredith said as Julia nodded. "We'll preserve the evidence and do the next thing."

She hung up and tucked the phone into her pocket then looked over at Julia. "Got a zip-top bag in your purse?"

"I'm fresh out," she said, "but I've probably got something in the car we can use. I'll go look. I'll do that while you make another pass through here and see if we've missed something that might be of value to the investigation."

Julia left Meredith in the apartment and made her way carefully down the rickety stairs then headed toward her car. Rummaging through the trunk, she found the oversized first aid kit Beau insisted she keep there.

Inside she found a plastic bag holding bandages that would work. She continued her search and came across a pair of gloves in the same kit. She stuffed everything back inside and zipped up the kit then took it with her back to the apartment.

Julia had just begun to ascend the staircase when she heard someone shout, "Are y'all not done yet? My cleaners will be here any minute."

She looked over her shoulder and saw the landlady standing there, hands on her hips. "We're collecting evidence to give to the police," she said. "It shouldn't take long."

"Evidence? What in the world? I want to see whatever it is you're taking out of there."

"Come on up," Julia said. "But keep in mind this could become a crime scene."

She frowned. "Does that mean I can't have it cleaned and rented again? I was thinking about putting it on one of those home rental sites, what with the location being right in the heart of things."

"Until someone from the police tells you otherwise, this apartment is yours to do with as you please," Julia said. "But we would be grateful if you let us remove anything that might help with our case."

"Yes, the case of the missing schnauzer," she said. "I saw that poor dear lady on the midday news. Terrible. Do you think my tenant had something to do with that?"

"We're here to try to determine that," Julia said.

The landlady paused a moment then shrugged. "I really want to get it rented again. Go ahead and take what you're going to need to take. Just let me see what you bring out."

Instead of following Julia upstairs, she disappeared into the garage below the apartment. Julia had reached the topmost step when the landlady came back out.

"I'll be right here waiting for you to check with me before you leave."

Julia turned around to see that the woman had donned sunglasses and a floppy white hat and was seated in a lawn chair in the shade of an oak tree beside the gate. "All right," she said. "We'll do that."

Julia stepped inside, brandishing the first aid kit, and made quick work of donning the gloves and scooping the deposit slip into the bag meant to hold bandages. As an afterthought, she returned to the bedside table, retrieved the contents of the top drawer and dumped them in the kit.

"As long as we don't touch any of that before we can find bags for them, I think they'll be fine," she said to Meredith. "Did you find anything else?"

"Just this." Meredith held up a folded slip of green paper between her thumb and forefinger. "It's a coupon for a half-price meal at the Square Deli. I tried not to touch it any more than necessary, but it was wedged under the sofa cushion, so I had to pull it out."

Julia looked at the folded coupon and then back at Meredith. "I know that place. It's near Johnson Square."

"Isn't that the area where you met Amy's boyfriend and his business partner this morning?" Meredith slipped the coupon into the first aid bag that Julia held open.

"It is." She looked at her watch. "I know yesterday we talked about going to the Downhome Diner for lunch, but what do you think about a change of plans?"

Chapter Thirteen

Kill Devil Hills, North Carolina
October 24, 1911

Oscar moved his deck chair out of the sun and allowed his gaze to follow a trio of birds skimming the water in front of his cottage. Orville Wright and his crew had been at it again today.

He'd watched the flying contraption rise up and soar twice already this afternoon, and he'd marveled at the length of time it stayed aloft. From his perch, Oscar had also seen the few false starts the machine had taken earlier, one of which he'd figured had doomed the craft.

But Orville and his men righted the upside-down craft and went right back at it. He glanced at his watch. This time he'd been up well over five minutes, almost ten.

One of the birds dipped its beak beneath the water's surface and emerged with a glistening fish while the other two squawked, either in complaint or approval.

He'd been postponing opening the letter from the Wilbert Trask Detective Agency. When Wilbert passed away suddenly last fall, Oscar had felt like his dream of finding Coraline died with him.

Likely the letter was an accounting of funds left or, as might be possible, funds owed. It had been six years since he'd walked into Trask's office and paid him to find Coraline. To open the letter would be to acknowledge that the search was over.

Oscar sighed and tore open the envelope. "Best get this over with."

Inside he found a letter from a fellow named Archibald Trask written on the letterhead of the Wilbert Trask Detective Agency.

Dear Mr. Bryant,

You have likely become aware that my father is no longer at the helm of the William Trask Detective Agency. With his death a few months ago, that responsibility has fallen to me—his son.

The letter went on to apologize for the delay in reaching out to him and to offer an accounting of funds still remaining in Oscar's account. Oscar had to read the last paragraph twice to make sure he was actually seeing the words correctly.

It is with some trepidation that I must inform you that there is information my father never shared with you. There is a Cora St. Germaine who is listed as the owner of a home on Oglethorpe Street in Savannah, Georgia. My father's records are vague, but it appears he knew of this woman for a number of years. It is possible he discounted her as the real Coraline and that is why you were never told. Since he cannot answer for himself, I felt it my duty to write you in regard to this matter. Please let me know how you wish to proceed.

Oscar read it again. Then again, aloud. If he had any neighbors close enough to hear him, they'd certainly think he'd lost his mind.

He laughed until he felt lightheaded, and then he sobered. Georgia. The woman who might be Coraline was living in Georgia.

The one state Oscar could not go without fear of arrest.

After several years of searching, the senior Trask had found a relative of the piano maker, a niece who still lived in the area. Oscar had deposited twice the amount he stole from her uncle into an account with her name on it and had written a heartfelt apology for what he'd done.

None of that changed the fact he might be a wanted man in the state of Georgia.

Oscar returned the letter to its envelope then tucked it into his shirt pocket, turned his back on the still-aloft flying machine, and went inside to the book-lined room he'd designated as his office. Unlike his Manhattan apartment, this beachside cottage was minuscule—just a few rooms, all of which had a view of the water or the dunes—but he'd never felt as much at home in New York as he did here.

Rather than waste time writing a letter, Oscar donned his hat and headed off to the telegraph office to respond. SEND ME THE INFORMATION STOP I WILL HANDLE THIS, he wrote to Trask's son.

The response came the next day. By then Oscar's plans were made.

Savannah, Georgia
November 2, 1911

"Well, sir, I'm Miss Havisham," Cora's boarder said from downstairs. "Since I don't know you from Adam, I'll not yet give you my Christian name, but I will deliver a message if you have one. So how can I help you today?"

"I'm looking for Miss St. Germaine."

That voice. No. It couldn't be. But it was. And he knew her name.

Her real name.

Cora inhaled a deep breath and then let it out slowly as she froze in her tracks on the second-floor landing of the boardinghouse, a stack of folded clean sheets slung over her arm. After all these years, she'd been found.

Despite Mr. Trask's warning, Cora hadn't thought it would really happen. But it had.

"Are you one of those racing fellows? This is a respectable boardinghouse, and the landlady does not rent to transients, even if they are here to participate in Mr. Vanderbilt's road race."

"I assure you, madam, I am not." He repeated the address to Miss Havisham. "Is that where I am?"

"It is," she told him. "But you look as if perhaps you were seeking another address."

"I, well..." A pause as a paper rustled. "No, that is the address I was given."

Cora glanced around and spied Ida making her way quietly down the staircase toward her. Ida Allen had been a combination of lady's maid to Mama and governess to Cora during the years when Daddy was alive and the St. Germaines employed a staff of a half dozen. Ida was often the shoulder Cora cried on when she'd had a disagreement with her parents or some other event had caused her grief.

Thus, when Cora returned to Savannah, Ida was the only person she trusted with the secret of where she'd been. Ida was a comfort to Cora through the years, and except for the fact that she persisted in trying to get Cora back on stage, she was also a good friend.

Ida had always managed to see through Cora's emotions. That ability had not diminished over the years. Though her expression looked troubled, Ida nodded to let Cora know she would remain quiet.

They stood side by side out of sight of the pair downstairs. "Somebody you don't want to see?" Ida whispered.

"Maybe," Cora said softly.

"Then it's a pity that back staircase was closed off during the last renovation, though I am grateful it allowed for indoor plumbing to be added on each floor."

Cora nodded. With this improvement to the house, any chance of escaping downstairs and out of the boardinghouse while Oscar was at the door was gone.

"Just let me see if she is available," Miss Havisham said, her lyrical voice rising. "And what was your name?"

Cora groaned. Ida gave her a sideways look.

There was a delay in responding. Then he said, "Clinton. Oliver Clinton."

Clinton? *Cora had only spent one evening with Oscar Bryant a decade ago, but there was no mistaking his voice as it echoed from her front door. So why was he using a name other than his own?*

While that was curious enough, more important was the fact that he currently stood on her doorstep. Cora had missed the first part of the conversation, having been changing bedsheets in the third-floor rooms when the door was opened.

The door closed, and Cora heard footsteps crossing the foyer below. When Miss Havisham looked up to spy her and Ida on the landing, she stopped short.

"Goodness me! You two scared the life out of me." She shook her head, causing her chin-length red ringlets to dance around her head.

While Miss Havisham was an avowed spinster and certainly no flapper, she had happily embraced the bobbed hairstyle that was generally seen on younger women. She also had an interest in knowing what went on in the boardinghouse as well as a strong flair for the dramatic, given that she'd been working on the same book of poetry ever since Cora moved into the building.

"I declare that handsome man wouldn't tell me a thing. I don't know how much you heard of our conversation, but he certainly wasn't giving me any information as to why he was here. Just kept asking for you." She paused. "You don't look pleased."

"I'm not particularly," Cora managed, settling the folded linen atop the chair on the landing. Then she added, "I was in the middle of changing sheets."

Once again, Miss Havisham nodded. "Yes, of course. Shall I tell him you're busy and ask again for a message?"

"Go on back upstairs," Ida said softly to Cora. "I can get rid of him if you want me to."

Though both options were tempting, ultimately there was no point in running or hiding. Cora had done both when she left her opera career behind, but in this case it would likely only be a temporary solution. Her letter from Mr. Trask's son letting her know he had kept the agency open after his father's death meant that Oscar's search for her would probably continue until he tired of looking for her.

"No, I'll speak to him," she said as she began her descent down the staircase. "Thank you, Miss Havisham."

Miss Havisham offered a broad smile and skittered over to a place behind the door. "Don't you worry, now. I'll be right here listening. All you need to do is give the signal, and I'll come to your rescue."

"Thank you, but that isn't necessary." Cora knew her tone was brisk, but at the moment it was all she could manage.

"If you're sure," Miss Havisham said, giving her a reluctant look as she moved toward the stairs.

"I am." Then she eased her tone. "I appreciate the offer, though."

"Are you sure?" Ida whispered.

Cora nodded. Displeasure showed on the older woman's face, but she said nothing more.

"I suppose I can just make my own bed then while you're at the door," Miss Havisham said when she'd stopped on the second riser up. "If it will help."

Ida rolled her eyes. Cora bit her lip for a moment.

"It would, thank you." Cora waited until Miss Havisham had taken her bed linens into her room and closed the door behind her. Likely it would open again as soon as Miss Havisham had determined that Cora was otherwise occupied.

"I'll stay right here and see she stays put if you'd like," Ida told her.

"That's not necessary, but thank you. I know you're busy."

"No more than you," she said. "But I'll go on down to the kitchen and stir the soup. I'll be just on the other side of that door if you need me."

Cora reached over to grasp Ida's hand. "Thank you."

Ida left her with a smile to disappear downstairs into the kitchen. Cora paused to center her thoughts and direct her prayers. Then she went to the door and opened it.

And there he was, standing on her doorstep.

Oscar Bryant had found her.

The years had been kind to the man. The smile she remembered was still there, and his eyes bore only slight traces of age at the corners. For a moment Cora wondered whether the lines were from laughter as befitting their name, and she hoped they were.

Today he wore a smart suit of dark gray wool, and his shoes bore the polished shine of a man who spent most of his time indoors. Even so, his face was tanned as if he did just the opposite.

Cora grasped the doorframe as she forced her expression to remain neutral. "Good morning. I understand you're looking for me."

The statement hung in the air between them. The color drained from Oscar's face.

"Yes, I, well, that is…" His voice sounded strained as he looked down at the fedora in his hands. Finally he shook his head and lifted his eyes to meet her gaze. "This is a boardinghouse? You're sure of it. I was told…"

She might have asked just who told him that, but Cora knew. Of all the private investigators in New York, he would have had to choose the same one she used.

The one who had certainly told him that Cora St. Germaine owned a boardinghouse on Oglethorpe Street in Savannah.

Cora considered telling him she knew exactly why he was there. Instead, she decided to continue the ruse and pretend not to recognize him until he forced her to do otherwise.

She couldn't say if the years had been kind to her—she tried not to look in the mirror more than necessary—but perhaps he wouldn't recognize her. After all, in her plain dress with her hair pinned up in a decidedly unfashionable style, she certainly bore little resemblance to the glamorous Coraline who had stood at center stage of Carnegie Hall all those years ago.

"If you're looking for lodgings, I happen to know there's an attic room available on Abercorn just around the corner," Cora said as evenly but cordially as she could manage. "You can't miss the signs. The whole building is for sale, but I understand they're still leasing the rooms in anticipation of the buyer taking the property rented out as it is. I suppose it's a risk, but Mrs. Partridge, the landlady, is nice, and the rent is lower than it is here. Although if you're here for the road race, you'll have a difficult time finding anyone to let a room."

Cora smiled then despite the butterflies in her stomach and the fact that she'd only remained upright by clutching the doorpost. She'd said far more than she intended, but it seemed wiser to talk than to allow him to finally get a word in and tell her why he was there.

Unfortunately, she'd run out of words.

Thus far, Oscar hadn't said anything. In fact, he looked as if he were no longer capable of speaking.

Mrs. Kassos from next door stepped out onto her porch to water her ferns. Though she said nothing as she lifted her copper watering can to the pot nearest Cora and Oscar, she made no attempt to hide her interest in the conversation going on a short distance away.

Or rather the conversation not currently going on.

Cora offered her neighbor a wave then returned her attention to Oscar. "Was there something else?"

A dangerous question, but standing here in silence was unnerving.

"So you're the landlady here?" He stepped back as if to check the number on the house. "At this address."

"I am. Is that all?" she asked briskly.

Was he pretending not to recognize her? Or did the obvious surprise etched on his features mean he did not know who she was after all? Perhaps old Mr. Trask had kept his word and burned all their correspondence before he died. That wouldn't explain how Oscar found her, but it might explain how he appeared to be so uncertain about it all.

"Yes ma'am," he said, his voice still straining as if the words were not easily formed. "I'll just go see about that attic room on Abercorn Street."

Cora mumbled some sort of response then said goodbye and closed the door. It wasn't until she leaned her back against the door, her heart racing, that she realized she'd given Oscar Bryant help in finding a place to stay in Savannah. The last thing she wanted was for him to remain in the city, let alone just around the corner.

Exhaling, Cora pushed away from the door. Immediately Ida opened the kitchen door. "What can I do?"

"Go tell Alma not to rent a room to Oscar—I mean, Oliver Bryant. He's on his way now, so you'll have to hurry."

Ida pulled off her apron. "I'll leave by the back door through the kitchen and take the alley. That'll see me there before he can find it."

Before Cora could thank her, Ida was gone. Cora moved toward the kitchen on legs that threatened to go out from beneath her.

"Hmmm... The name Oscar seemed to come out of nowhere."

Her footsteps faltered. Cora looked over her shoulder at Miss Havisham, who was now perched on the stairs halfway between the first and second floor.

"I misspoke," Cora said, averting her eyes.

"Seemed like you two had something going there other than just a conversation about a room at a boardinghouse." She shrugged. "Before he knocked, I saw him standing in the boulevard for a good ten minutes before he worked up the courage to come over and knock on the door. I think he was looking for you and not a room."

Cora squared her shoulders and faced down the older woman with the last of her backbone. "I'm sure I don't know what you're talking about."

With that, she stepped into the kitchen and allowed the door to swing closed behind her. Ignoring the bread that was rising in the bowl on the table, she sank onto the nearest chair and closed her eyes.

Now what, Lord?

Chapter Fourteen

THE SQUARE CAFE WAS RELATIVELY quiet and devoid of tourists this afternoon as Meredith and Julia slid into the booth next to the window.

The interior of the café was decorated to match its name. Squares of all colors were painted in random places across the pale gray walls, and each booth featured a square lamp hanging overhead, its shade decorated in a similar design.

Meredith had tried calling Stephanie again using the number Brian Duffy had given them. There had been no answer and no indication that a voice mail had been set up. Rather, when she called the second time, a recording announced that the phone was no longer in service.

It was clear that Stephanie was lying low.

"It's pretty quiet here," Meredith said as she reached for one of the menus stacked at the end of the table.

"To be fair, it is late for lunch on a weekday," Julia said.

"I blame the taco truck over by the office building," a woman wearing navy trousers and a matching blazer over a T-shirt with the café's logo said as she approached with two glasses of water. "The only day we're not busy is Taco Tuesday. What'll you have to drink today, ladies?"

Julia glanced at the name tag the woman wore before answering. It said GINGER LOWE, MANAGER.

Exactly the person they needed to interview.

Julia grinned. "Water is fine. Thank you," she said, and Meredith nodded in agreement.

A few minutes later Ginger returned to take their orders then hurried off to the kitchen. Julia watched her go and then turned her attention to Meredith.

"She's the manager. When she comes back with our lunch, I think we should ask her about the coupons."

Meredith nodded. "We need to play it casual, though. At this point we can't rule anyone out. Someone folded that coupon and possibly hid it in the sofa cushions. It could very well mean something."

"Okay," Julia said. "Go for it, and I'll jump in if I think of any questions that you haven't asked."

"Or to play good cop, bad cop if we need to," Meredith said with a chuckle.

"You watch too many police shows, Meredith. We have never played good cop, bad cop, and I don't know if I even know how to do that," Julia protested.

"Then you can be the bad cop," she said. "I'll be the good cop who makes her confess."

"I think you've been out in the heat too long," Julia said.

Meredith laughed. "I'm teasing. Besides, everyone knows the bad cop is the one who makes the perpetrator confess."

When Ginger returned with their food, Meredith offered a smile. "It looks absolutely delicious. Say, I wonder if you have a minute."

Ginger looked doubtful but shrugged. "I've got time. How can I help you?"

"I'm curious about the half-price coupons you have."

"Are you asking for the discount now?" she asked. "The coupon clearly states that you have to show the coupon before you order. Otherwise you lose the right to the discount."

"No, nothing like that," Meredith said. "I'm just curious where people get those."

She sighed. "We had a deal with a tour company to pass them out. If you buy a tour, you get a coupon. Well, actually you get an assortment of them, ours being one of them."

"You said *had*," Julia interjected. "Does that mean you're no longer handing out coupons through the tour company?"

"They're still handing them out," Ginger said with obvious annoyance, "but I elected not to renew our agreement. I didn't see an uptick in customers, though our regulars started coming in and using the coupons." She shook her head. "That's not how it was supposed to work."

"How was it supposed to work?" Meredith asked.

"Like I said, you buy a tour and you get a coupon. It was supposed to get us new customers from the tourist crowd. I suspect they weren't just handing them out to the people who rode in a carriage behind a horse for two hours listening to a history lesson."

"Which tour company were you working with?" Julia asked.

"Travel Through Time Tours," she said.

Meredith picked up her sandwich as if she planned to take a bite then paused. "And did you deal with anyone in particular there?"

Ginger shook her head again. "Everything was done by emails. Why?"

Meredith reached into her purse and handed Ginger her card. "I'm Meredith Bellefontaine, and this is Julia Foley. We're from Magnolia Investigations, and we're looking into a case."

Ginger accepted the card then glanced down to read it before looking back up at Meredith, her eyes narrowed. "What would your case have to do with my coupon and Travel Through Time Tours?"

"That's what we're trying to figure out," Julia said.

"It has to do with a missing loved one," Meredith said. "We're hoping to locate the loved one, and as we were tracking down clues, we stumbled onto your coupon. So if you could help, we'd appreciate it," she added with a smile.

Ginger's tense expression eased. "I see. Well, I wish I could help, but all I know is that they have an email address and a phone number. The phone number is on all their ads, so it wouldn't help if I gave it to you, since you can easily find it." She paused. "But honestly all I did was try a promotion that didn't work out. I don't know anything about missing loved ones."

"Thank you," Meredith said. "If you think of anything, would you give us a call?"

"Sure, yes." She glanced down at the table then back at Meredith, who was happily eating her pastrami on rye. "Now I need to get back to the kitchen. Enjoy your lunch."

As Ginger hurried away, Meredith beamed. "See how well that worked?"

Julia stabbed at her Cobb salad with her fork. "How well what worked?"

"The good cop, bad cop routine."

Julia laughed. "I wasn't trying to do that."

"And yet I was the good cop and you were—"

"Okay," Julia said. "Maybe I was a little more firm with her than you were. I'm just glad we have the name of the tour company. Did you get the sense she was trying to hide anything? Because I didn't."

"No, I think she's telling us what she knows. Or at least I hope that's the case." Meredith shrugged. "This pastrami sandwich is delicious."

When they were finished with their late lunch, Julia followed Meredith outside. As they made their way to the car, Julia looked over at the Manger Building, where she'd started the day before.

Seth was paying them a lot of money to find Bosco. The money he'd spent on ads and on getting Amy on television and radio had to be substantial. Surely he wouldn't also be part of the problem.

Later as Julia sat at her desk, she reviewed her notes of her meeting with Seth. Nothing he had said raised any red flags. He truly seemed to love Amy, and he was adamant that he wanted Bosco returned to her.

Her meeting with Kenton, however, raised more questions than gave answers. On the one hand, he seemed intelligent, loyal to Seth, and willing to help. On the other hand, he admitted he had issues with Amy being with Seth. What Julia couldn't decide was whether that dislike had fueled some sort of plot to make Amy miserable by taking her dog.

Julia leaned back in her chair and pinched the bridge of her nose. No matter how she tried, she couldn't make sense of the pieces of this puzzle. Nor could she shake the feeling that neither Seth Stevenson nor Kenton Hollis had told her everything they knew about the situation.

She turned the page to look at the notes she'd made regarding Woof Walk. Brian Duffy was a bit of an odd duck, but he didn't seem like someone who would steal a dog. As far as she could tell, there was no connection between Duff and Amy or Seth.

Julia switched her attention to the report on Phil Weber that Carmen had left on her desk while they were gone. The man's record was spotless. Not even a speeding ticket. She turned the page. Carmen had printed a page from Weber's local paper in Connecticut. The date was Saturday the day after Bosco disappeared.

Her eyes trailed down the page to the photograph and article that Carmen had circled. "RETIREE WINS FRIDAY FISHING FUN ALL-DAY TOURNAMENT AGAIN," the headline said. Beneath that line was a photograph of an elderly man smiling from his wheelchair, one hand holding up a large fish and the other lifting a trophy.

"Oh," Julia said as she scanned the article. Phil Weber's alibi was printed right there in the *Saturday Morning Standard*. He'd spent the whole day fishing many hundreds of miles away. But all that proved was that he didn't take Bosco himself. He could have been the one who paid Stephanie to drop the leash.

Julia returned her thoughts to Stephanie Sterling. Carl had been off the day before, and a substitute had delivered the mail in his place. Until she spoke to Carl, she had no way to contact Stephanie. It was frustrating, but there was nothing she could do.

Thoughts of Stephanie reminded her that she'd brought the first aid kit inside but hadn't opened it yet. When she got home tonight, she would bag each item using fresh gloves and zip-top bags just as Wally instructed.

She glanced at her watch. Though it seemed as though she'd only been back from lunch for a short while, it was after four o'clock. Of course they hadn't left the café until after two thirty, so in truth she hadn't spent much time at the office this afternoon.

Carmen appeared in the doorway. "I'm making coffee and heating up a cinnamon roll. Want some?"

"Thanks but no," Julia said. "I think I'm going to take these notes and go home to transcribe them. I'm tired."

"Of course you're tired. Get some rest. Oh, but don't forget to watch Amy on the news tonight. She's going to be interviewed about losing Bosco. I sent you a text about it earlier."

"Oh, that's right." Julia closed her laptop and tucked it into her bag. "Maybe all these appearances Amy is doing will help us find Bosco. Surely someone out there has a clue that will lead us to him."

Carmen smiled. "I'm glad you and Meredith took this job. I know finding a lost dog isn't the typical kind of case that Magnolia Investigations would work on, but Bosco means a lot to Amy."

"I'm hoping that finding the bank receipt means we're one step closer to finding the dog."

"I hope so too," Carmen said. "Are you sure you don't want to take a cinnamon roll for the road?"

Julia laughed. "Thank you but no, although if you wouldn't mind, I would be forever grateful if you would grab a Diet Dr Pepper for me. I'll claim it on my way out."

"I can do that."

"Thank you," she called after Carmen.

After collecting everything she needed to work at home tonight, Julia hitched her computer bag and purse over her shoulder and snatched up the first aid kit. She walked down the hall to let Meredith know she was leaving and found her partner on the phone.

Julia gestured to her bags and waved, indicating she would be gone for the day. Meredith nodded and returned to her call.

She headed to the kitchen, where she found Carmen setting her drink on the counter. "Here you go," Carmen said. "Ready for the road."

"Thank you." Julia smiled at her.

"Oh," Carmen said, "I almost forgot. Seth called to say he sent a team over to the neighborhood around Forsyth Park to search for Bosco. They didn't find anything, but he's considering widening the search tomorrow."

Julia nodded. "At this point, I'm not going to discourage him from doing that. I truly don't know what'll work and what's just a wild-goose chase."

The phone rang, and Carmen hurried away to answer it. Julia juggled her bags until she was able to retrieve the Diet Dr Pepper from the counter and still manage to shut the back door behind her.

She was moving toward her car when she saw a man walking through the parking lot toward her. It was Brian Duffy.

He glanced around before he waved in her direction. "I thought I might find you here."

Julia unlocked her car and situated her bags, keeping an eye on the man as she did so. "Generally people come to the front door of Magnolia Investigations. Why would you think you'd find me in the parking lot?"

"It's not important. What is important is the news I got regarding Stephanie Sterling. Were you able to talk to her today?"

"No," she said. "The number didn't work, and she's moved from the address we found."

He leaned against Julia's car and grinned. "Well then, I have good news for you."

"What's that?"

"Stephanie had a job interview today, and afterward the guy made some calls to check her references and job history. I could have been a jerk about it, but I decided if I was nice maybe I'd be able to find out more about what she's up to now, you know?"

"I guess that makes sense," Julia said. "Were you able to find out anything?"

"I found out she applied for a job at a pet store."

Julia inhaled sharply. "Really. That's interesting."

"I thought so. So anyway, she starts tomorrow. The guy just called me back and told me he hired her on my word." Duff chuckled. "I hope he's not mad when she turns out to be a total ditz for him like she was for me."

Julia studied him a moment. "You're still certain that Stephanie let Bosco pull free, aren't you?"

He scratched his head. "Certain isn't exactly the right word. Let's just say I'm pretty sure of it. Look, she's an airhead, but she's a good kid. Her uncle vouched for her when I hired her, and she was that little dog's regular walker for several months with no problems." Duff paused. "Anyway, I wrote down the address of the pet shop and the name of the guy who called me in case you wanted it."

Julia accepted the paper from Duff. "Thank you."

Duff moved back from Julia's car but made no motion to walk away. Instead, he stood there expectantly.

"Is there something else?"

"Probably not," he said, "but I'll mention it anyway. About a month ago the Bananas had a Bring Your Pet to the Game day. Bosco was there."

"With Seth or Amy?"

"No, with Kenton. He wasn't happy about it either. He complained the whole game. Said he was doing this for Seth but not for Amy. Said the dog wasn't a bad sort but he hated being told what to do like that. Said he didn't go to Harvard to dog-sit."

"Okay. Why would Seth ask him to take a dog to a local baseball game?"

"One of Seth's companies was sponsoring the seventh-inning stretch. Seth couldn't be there because he had some event with Amy already planned. The management of the team wanted a dog with Kenton when he went onto the field. They had this great idea to have Bosco take the baseball from the pitcher's mound to home plate— sort of a puppy first pitch. It was great. The fans loved it."

"I'm sure it was adorable," Julia said. "How long ago was that?"

"About a month or so. I'm thinking June at the latest." He shrugged. "You can look on the Bananas event calendar online and see when it was. They've got all the special stuff listed there."

"Thank you, Duff," Julia said. Then she had another thought. "How does it work when you sponsor the seventh-inning stretch? Is there anything more involved than just the traditional song?"

"Oh yeah," Duff said. "There's usually something special. For this particular game they passed out ice cream sandwiches."

"Really? Why ice cream sandwiches?"

"Because the sponsor was Sally's Ice Cream Shop," he said.

The name rang a bell, but why? Julia said goodbye to Duff and drove home pondering the question. Later that evening, with the zip-top bags spread in front of her and the contents of the first aid kit ready to be bagged, it hit her where she'd heard the name.

Using her gloves, Julia dug into the depths of the kit to retrieve the pink pen she found in Stephanie Sterling's nightstand.

There on the side was the logo she remembered. The logo for Sally's Ice Cream Shop.

And with that, a link between Kenton Hollis or Seth Stevenson and Stephanie Sterling was established. It was a tenuous link that might amount to nothing—after all, maybe Stephanie just liked ice cream and accidentally brought home a pen after signing a receipt.

Or maybe Stephanie and Kenton were in this dognapping together.

Chapter Fifteen

THE NEXT MORNING JULIA HAD just stepped out of the shower when she heard Beau calling her. She stuck her head out of the bathroom to see what he wanted.

"That woman you're working for—the one who lost her dog. She's going to be on the morning show in a few minutes."

"Oh that's right," Julia said. "I was going to watch her interview last night but got wrapped up in research and completely forgot."

She toweled off and slipped into her clothes then hurried downstairs where Beau had the television turned on. A commercial ended, and the local weatherman's face filled the screen. Julia poured a cup of coffee as news of a disturbance in the tropics became the top story of the segment.

Then came the smiling faces of the morning news team, Tina Blake and Tom Williams. Known as Tina and Tom, their faces were plastered over half the buses in Savannah and on billboards all over town.

A moment later, Amy Bryant was introduced. Though she had obviously been through hair and makeup at the station, she still looked natural as she spoke.

Abruptly the camera cut to Tina, a perky blond with a broad smile. "We will hear more from Amy Bryant of Amy's Bakery and

Bistro on the Thursday morning edition of *Savanah Morning News* when we come back from our commercial break."

Beau settled beside Julia on the sofa. "Is that your new client?"

She nodded. "Her boyfriend is paying, but she's the dog's owner."

"Are you sure?"

Julia tore her eyes from the television screen to look at her husband. "What do you mean?"

He shrugged and took a sip of his coffee. "Just a thought. Maybe the dog doesn't actually belong to her. I saw it in a movie once."

She gave him a sideways look. "Were you watching one of those made-for-television Christmas movies again?"

"Maybe." He gave her his signature half grin that she loved so much. "In the movie everyone thought the dog belonged to the lady who lost him, but instead the dog really belonged to the guy who'd been looking for him for almost a year."

"Let me guess, the guy moved in next door. He's a writer and has been working on his book but is blocked because he misses his dog. So he moves to a new town next door to the…" She put her finger to her chin. "Give me a minute. Oh yes, next to the single kindergarten teacher who was given the pup by…"

At her husband's astonished expression, Julia held up her hand to ward off any help with the remainder of the plot. "Okay, she was given the dog by the grateful parent of a student she helped to learn to read. The parent works at a dog rescue, and the dog was found and thought abandoned last Christmas Eve. Dog gets loose and goes next door to appear at the writer's door. Writer is reunited with his long-lost pet and now can finish his book. But wait. It isn't that easy."

Beau shook his head. "Is it ever?"

"Well, no, because there's a lawyer who has been trying to marry her ever since they were college sweethearts and he has other plans. He's going to sue the writer neighbor and get the dog back so she will finally love him. It works perfectly until the kindergarten teacher and the writer fall in love, embrace each other and the dog on the perfectly manicured lawn between their very expensive homes, and vow to give little Freckles a home for life together. Cue the snow."

Beau laughed, and Julia joined him. "Freckles?" he asked.

She shrugged. "It was the first name I thought of."

He looked over at the sliver of sunshine where their rescue cat was sunning herself and ignoring them. "Glad she didn't think of that when you came to live with us, Jack."

The cat's name was actually Bunny, but owing to the feline's long legs, Beau had christened her with the nickname of Jackrabbit. Thus, in his eyes, she'd become Jack for short.

She looked over at them, yawned, and went back to sleep. "So much for caring what we're saying," Julia said.

"Oh, she cares," he told her. "Just wait until you've gone to work. Jack and I have great chats on deep topics. We solve world peace and other important issues while you're gone."

"In other words, you contemplate life's most important subjects while you're curled up to nap together."

"Maybe." Beau pretended offense and then laughed. "No more than once a day, and I always set an alarm so I'm awake when you get home. I do give myself an extra fifteen minutes if I've cut the grass that day. It gets hot in the summer."

"Well, of course," she told him.

He leaned over to give her a kiss on the cheek. Julia grinned.

"Anyway," Beau continued, "I'm no detective, but if I were you I would check that out."

Julia picked up the phone and dialed Carmen. When she answered, Julia hurried to apologize. "I'm sorry for calling you before work, but I need to know if you have something before you come in."

"What's that?" Carmen answered.

A truck commercial was blaring, and Beau used the remote to mute the sound. She mouthed a thanks.

"Remember you told me about how Amy wrote that recipe down for you on a copy of her dog's AKC registration the day you first met?"

"Sure," she said. "It was a pasta dish. I have it memorized."

"Do you still have the written version? The actual one that Amy gave you?"

Carmen paused only a moment. "It's stuck in one of my recipe books, so I would have to look for it, but I'm pretty sure I do."

"Would you mind doing that and bringing it in if you find it? Don't worry about being late if it takes a while to find the recipe. I really would like to see that paper."

"Sure, no problem," she said. "Is that all?"

"Yes, that's it. And thank you." Julia hung up and set the phone aside. "Okay, we'll know soon."

Beau unmuted the sound just in time for the camera to zoom in on Amy holding an oversized photo of Bosco. Julia noticed that over her jeans and white T-shirt she wore a green apron trimmed in red and bearing the logo of Amy's Bakery and Bistro.

Kenton Hollis's words echoed through Julia's mind. *Follow the money.*

She sighed.

The blond anchor's smile filled the screen and then the camera pulled back to show both of them again. "Before we get down to business, I have to say I've had Amy's cinnamon rolls." Tina flashed that smile at the camera again. "They are delicious. And thank you, by the way, for bringing some for our crew."

"You're welcome, Tina."

The remainder of the interview was a rehash of the facts surrounding Bosco's disappearance. Likely at the insistence of the television station's legal team, there was no mention of the details of a dog walker from Woof Walk.

"So the day started with a nice walk in the park for Bosco," Tina said, "and turned into one of tragic loss and unimaginable sorrow."

"Wow," Beau said. "Someone worked hard on that line. No way she just came up with that on the fly."

"Maybe she takes deep philosophical naps and these things come to her," Julia said with a giggle as Beau shook his head.

"Yes, Tina," Amy said, her voice wavering. "His dog bed by the window is empty, and there's no one to bark when the delivery truck parks out front. It's just…"

Julia couldn't help but notice that someone had taken the photo from Amy and given her a tissue.

"…just so quiet and it makes me so sad," Amy continued, wiping her nose.

"Folks, help Amy find Bosco," Tina said as the dog's photograph appeared on the screen along with a tip line phone number and an email address to report possible sightings.

"That's not your office number," Beau said.

"Or an email we created," Julia added. "It might have been help-ful to know about this tip line."

The camera returned to Tina and Amy. "I understand you've got some plans to heighten awareness of this campaign to bring Bosco home."

"Yes," Amy said. "First of all, I would love it if you would use the hashtag we've set up for this purpose. It's hashtag BringBoscohometotheBistro."

"Did you all get that?" Tina asked with a grin before she repeated the hashtag. "Is there anything else?"

"Yes," Amy said. "As I told you off camera, I've been baking a lot since Bosco's been gone. That translates to more food than I can sell at Amy's Bistro and Bakery during our regular hours. So I'm doing two things."

Tina looked into the camera. "I cannot wait to find out what she's doing, can you?"

The camera returned to Amy and she continued, "First of all, since I can't bear to be alone in my apartment in the evenings, I've decided to open Amy's Bistro and Bakery for limited dinner service Thursday through Saturday nights."

"Well, that's convenient," Beau muttered. "Seeing as today is Thursday, which would make tonight their first night to be open for dinner. Pretty good free publicity if you ask me."

Follow the money.

"Oh, that is exciting. I understand our lifestyle reporter Cozy Vanderwegen will be reporting from the bistro on our evening news. And what's the other thing?" Tina asked.

"I'm opening an online cookie store as of this morning. In honor of my sweet Bosco, we'll only be offering one style of cookie this week."

"Show our viewers that cookie," Tina said, and the image of a sugar cookie decorated to look like a black schnauzer with a red collar appeared on the screen. "Oh that is darling," could be heard as the image disappeared and Amy returned.

"All proceeds from the cookie sale will go to animal charities," she said. "And if you use the coupon code 'BringBoscohometotheBistro,' you'll get free shipping and an extra cookie."

Tina's face appeared on the screen. "I know I'm going to make use of that coupon code. I've had Amy's cookies, and they are fabulous." She paused. "Amy, before we let you go, is there anything else you would like to add?"

The camera moved to Amy, who was now devoid of tissue and held Bosco's picture again. "Bringing Bosco home is more important than anything else. If you see a little dog that looks like my Bosco, stop and ask questions. Take a video. Be nosy."

"Good advice," Tina said from off screen.

Amy looked down and wiped her face with her free hand and then straightened again. "I would like to say to whoever has Bosco that the eyes of Savannah are watching and so are the detectives of Magnolia Investigations. Julia and Meredith will find you if someone else doesn't find you first. Please, just return Bosco, and we won't press charges."

Tina's face returned to the screen. As she repeated the contact information that had been previously given, Beau reached for the remote and switched off the television.

"At least she gave you and Meredith a nice shout-out there at the end," he said.

The phone rang again. This time it was Carmen. Julia put her on speaker as she rose and padded to the kitchen to deposit her coffee cup in the sink.

"Okay, Boss," Carmen said. "I've got the recipe. Did you see Amy on the morning show? She did great, didn't she?"

"She did," Julia said. "I'm hoping this interview will generate lots of leads. Just one thing, though. Do you know anything about the phone number and email address they put up on the screen?"

"It was news to me," Carmen said.

Beau joined Julia in the kitchen and placed his cup next to hers in the sink. He moved over to the breakfast table to pick up the newspaper he had left there.

"Okay, so it's nothing our office is doing, then?" Julia asked her.

"Nope," Carmen said. "Want me to get the scoop from Amy on it?"

"That would be helpful," Julia said. "We may need to coordinate efforts with whoever else she's hired to work on the return of the dog. I don't understand why she didn't tell us about this. I didn't like finding out with the rest of Savannah."

"It'll be Seth's doing, I'm sure. My guess is she didn't know until right before she went in for the interview, but I'll check on it. He would do anything for her and her business."

"Anything?" Julia asked.

"Well, sure, I mean as long as it's legal. Seth is a straight-arrow guy, or has been as long as I've known him." She paused. "Now his buddy Kenton? Whole other story. I don't think he likes her."

Julia's gaze met Beau's. The expression on his face told Julia they were likely thinking the same thing. "You're right about that. He admitted to me that he doesn't."

"Of course not. He's jealous that his best friend has a girlfriend and he doesn't," Carmen said. "At least that's my impression. Anyway, I'm on my way to the office. Just thought I'd let you know I have the recipe."

"Thanks, Carmen. I'll be in soon."

Julia ended the call. Then she dialed the number that she'd seen on the television screen.

After two rings, she heard, "Hi! This is Amy. Thank you for calling the Bring Bosco home to the Bistro hotline. If you have a tip to report, press one. If you would like to know what today's soup is or anything related to our bistro menu or to place an order, press two."

Julia hung up with a sigh. "Too bad there's not another option," she muttered.

Beau put his paper down and looked at her, his brows raised.

"The answering machine said to press one if you have a tip and two if you want to know the day's menu. I want another one. 'If you think Seth set this all up to get great publicity for Amy's cookies, press three.'"

Beau moved to close the distance between them. "I have no doubt that very soon you and Meredith will know whether that's true or not." He gave her a hug. "As for me, I think I'll go see if the fish are biting."

Julia grinned and watched her husband stroll outside, newspaper under his arm. As if he knew she was watching, Beau glanced back over his shoulder and blew her a kiss.

Chapter Sixteen

Alma perched on the edge of her chair and gave Cora an expectant look. The weather was mild and sunny, so the ladies were enjoying a visit on the porch.

"Well, what do you think?"

Cora tasted the pound cake her friend had brought. "It's delicious."

Her eyes narrowed. "But?"

She shrugged as she took another bite and chewed slowly. Then she put the fork down. "Maybe a little more cardamom?"

"Yes, of course. I'll do that." She sat back in her chair. "I've been meaning to ask you something, Cora." Alma paused only a moment before continuing. "Ever since Ida gave me that message telling me not to rent a room to Mr. Clinton, I've been curious why. Ida didn't know."

"Because I haven't said," Cora told her. "I have my reasons, but I would rather not discuss them."

"All right, I won't press you right now."

Cora knew the careful addition of those last two words meant that Alma would come back to the topic at a later date and begin the questions where she left off. She nodded and said, "Thank you."

"But I do have some news."

Her expression seemed innocent enough, but Cora had a feeling her words might not be. She picked up her teacup and took a sip. Made from tea grown by Dr. Shepard at his Pinehurst Tea Plantation near Summerville, South Carolina, it was better than any brew she'd had in all her travels around the world.

"I asked your opinion about the cake because I have a special use for it." Alma punctuated the statement with a smile and a shrug. "I—or rather we—will be offering it as our dessert in the restaurant that will be opening at the boarding-house. And by we, I mean Mr. Clinton and me."

The teacup rattled as Cora placed it back on the saucer. She looked down and realized her hands were shaking.

Oblivious, Alma continued. "When I wouldn't rent him the attic room, Mr. Clinton went to the owner and bought the whole place. Can you feature it? I heard he paid cash for it, but you know how the help likes to gossip. My maid's sister works for the chairman of the Savannah Bank and Trust Company over on the corner of Bay and Drayton Streets. You know, the bank that's building that showplace over on Bull Street?"

"Yes, I know the one," Cora said, struggling to keep her voice steady.

What she didn't share was that the Savannah Bank and Trust Company held what was left of the earnings she'd accrued during her years with the opera. Since the funds were deposited into an account that had once belonged to Mama and Papa, there would be no link there between Cora St. Germaine and the missing opera singer Coraline.

"Well, anyway," Alma continued, "the rumor is that Mr. Clinton went right to the banker's home and made him an offer in cash for the boardinghouse on the stipulation that the sale go through in one week's time. It must have, because here we are."

"Well," Cora managed as she spied Mrs. Kassos stepping onto her porch next door. "How nice for him. Would you like more tea?"

"I really couldn't." Alma rose. "I am incredibly busy."

Cora rose to her feet. "Let me get your cake and plate."

She held up both hands. "Oh no. Don't you worry about it. Serve that cake to your boarders tonight and return the plate tomorrow. There'll be plenty more at the restaurant when it opens, and it'll taste even better because it'll have the addition of cardamom."

"You know, Alma," Cora said. "About that. I'm thinking that what the cake really needs isn't cardamom at all."

Her friend frowned. "It isn't?"

"No, I think perhaps an extra dash of vanilla and some nutmeg might do the trick."

Alma gave her a thoughtful look. "Vanilla and nutmeg. Yes, all right. That's what I'll do."

After bidding Cora goodbye, Alma set off down the street. She hadn't yet turned the corner when Ida stepped out onto the porch.

"What's that Clinton fellow up to, Cora?"

"I wish I knew," she told her. "And then again, I'm glad I don't. I'd rather have nothing to do with him."

"So you said before." Ida gave her a look. "And you're still not saying why."

Cora placed the dessert plates and teacups on the tray and picked it up. "Exactly. Now would you mind holding the door open for me so I can get these back to the kitchen?"

"It's about your singing, isn't it?" Ida asked softly when they were safely in the kitchen with the door closed behind them. "He knows you from back then, I can feel it. This is why you need to just let that voice loose again. It's been bottled up inside you, and you hide that need to sing, just like you hide who you were when you were singing."

Cora carefully placed the dishes in the sink then stood very still. The rebuttal she'd formed in her mind fell flat before she allowed the words to be spoken.

"Okay then," Ida muttered, edging Cora away from the sink so she could attend to the washing up, "but you mark my words. The Lord isn't going to let that voice of yours stay hidden. You're hiding your light under a bushel basket, Cora St. Germaine. One of these days He is going to step in and see that it's used for the purpose for which He gave it to you."

"And what is that?" Cora asked as she leaned against the table, arms folded over her chest and a dozen other responses swirling in her mind.

"You'll know when the time comes." Ida looked up from her work to meet Cora's gaze. "The Bible says in the sixteenth verse of Psalm 59, "'But I will sing of thy power; yea, I will sing aloud of thy mercy in the morning: for thou hast been my defence and refuge in the day of my trouble.'"

Her old friend's eyes shifted to look out the window for a moment before she returned her attention to Cora. "When it happens, you won't be able to stop it. And it's going to bring comfort and hope to someone. Mark my words."

Chapter Seventeen

CARMEN WASN'T AT HER DESK when Julia arrived, but she could hear her talking to someone in the conference room. She left her purse and the first aid kit in her office then poked her head in the door and saw Carmen on her phone, standing amid the mountain of charity boxes.

"No, they'll be gone today, but thanks so much for helping. I'd still be stuffing boxes if you hadn't given up your time."

Silence. Then she laughed. "Okay, maybe you did distract me with your videos, but only you could make packing boxes fun."

So she was speaking to Chase. Julia smiled. It was nice to see Meredith's son around the office. She knew Meredith felt the same. That he got along well with Carmen was a bonus.

Carmen turned around and saw Julia standing there. "Gotta go." She hung up then shrugged. "Delivery was moved to this afternoon."

"No problem," Julia said. "We won't need the conference room today."

"I made a copy of the recipe," Carmen said. "It's on your desk."

"Both sides?" Julia asked.

Carmen looked confused. "No, just the recipe."

"Would you mind making a copy of the other side?"

"Sure. I can do that."

Julia stepped back to let her pass then followed Carmen up to the front of the building, waving at Meredith as she passed her office. She waited while Carmen retrieved a ragged slip of paper with a torn corner and tomato sauce stains along one side and turned it over to place it on her scanner. A moment later, Julia had a somewhat pristine version of an AKC registration certificate.

As she was looking at it, Carmen said, "I called Amy and asked her if Bosco was microchipped. She said he was. So if he's found or turned in to a shelter or vet, they should be able to find Amy's information through the chip and contact her." She shook her head. "But that doesn't help us if someone doesn't want him found."

Julia smiled at her. "But that's good thinking, Carmen. It's an important detail to know."

Carmen returned her smile. "Just trying to think like a private investigator. Oh," she said sharply. "One more thing. You asked me to do a search on Dan Bell, Seth's old classmate. I finished that one this morning and emailed what I found to you and Meredith. Do you want me to print it out like I did for that Weber guy who's suing over the recipe card?"

"No, I'll read mine on my computer." Julia headed for her office with the American Kennel Club information in hand, pausing while Carmen was still in view. "Knowing Amy as well as you do, Carmen, who do you think took Bosco?"

"I've thought a lot about that. I just don't know. I guess it's because I can't figure out the why of it. If I knew why then I would know who." She shrugged. "You've met her. Amy doesn't have an enemy."

"Other than the man who wants his Julia Child recipe card back—though his alibi is airtight. And the woman with the restaurant next door who isn't happy about the business she believes the bistro has been taking away from her." She paused. "Those are just the ones who don't like Amy. I haven't even begun to look into the ones who don't like Seth."

Carmen sighed. "Yeah, I'm sure there are a lot of people when you put all those names together. Oh! I also had a call from Kenton. He'll be emailing that list you asked him for as soon he can. He said he's been busy."

"I've been looking forward to seeing his list of suspects," said Julia.

"I've got a suspect," Meredith said, padding down the hall toward them. "Remember Seth's high school nemesis?"

Julia chuckled. "You've already kicked off your shoes, so I'm guessing you've been hard at work this morning."

Meredith grinned. "Actually, the cute shoes I bought on sale turned out not to be as comfortable as they are stylish. I've discovered that the hard way. But I'll manage. So anyway, this Dan Bell guy? The address you were given for him is correct. He owns his own tractor trailer and does long and short hauls. Mostly short."

"So he keeps his own time and isn't tied down to an office job. There's no one looking over his shoulder or keeping tabs on what he's doing."

"Exactly. And I called the pet store where Stephanie is supposed to begin work today. They open at noon on Thursdays and close at eight."

"So we can check out Dan before we go see what Stephanie's story is," Julia said.

"And check out Amy's pasta recipe," Carmen reminded her.

At Meredith's confused look, Julia nodded toward her office. "Come sit down, and I'll fill you in."

Meredith followed Julia down the hall into her office. Julia settled onto her chair, and Meredith took a seat across from her.

"Okay, so let's start with this recipe," Julia said. "I could give you the longer version, but it has to do with a made-for-television Christmas movie, a writer, and a kindergarten teacher."

At Meredith's confused expression, Julia held up the registration page Carmen had printed and studied it. "Okay, here it is."

Her eyes stalled at the line stating who owned Bosco. Or, more specifically, King Bosco III of the Bramblewoods.

Julia handed the page to Meredith. The moment her partner reached the surprising line, she looked up at her.

"Bosco doesn't belong to Amy."

"No, he doesn't," Julia said.

Meredith placed the paper on the desk between them and met Julia's gaze. "Who is S. E. Winter?"

"My guess is Suzanne Winter," Julia said. "As in Sooz of Sooz's Restaurant."

"The next-door neighbor? No." Meredith shook her head. "But she's mad at Amy. Why would she give her a dog?"

"Good question," Julia said. "And why wouldn't Amy tell us that? She did mention that Sooz's nephew designed custom collars, and she let them use Bosco to try them out."

Meredith held up her hand. "Before you go any further, get your notebook out. We're adding to that suspect list. We need to know who Sooz Winter's nephew is."

Julia nodded and did as Meredith said.

"Without looking at that stack of papers and adding anyone else, look at the list and tell me who stands out to you."

Julia scanned the page. "Kenton Hollis for one," she said. "But I could make a case for all of them, or else they would be eliminated."

"We haven't talked about Phil Weber."

Julia sat back in the chair. "Did you look at the report Carmen printed for us? He's got an airtight alibi. He was at a fishing tournament all day on Friday. That doesn't mean he might not be the money guy, but he certainly didn't come down here and take the dog himself."

"Okay, well, I guess we tell the cops about him and let them check out his finances," Meredith said. "Moving on, I had something else on my to-do list this morning. Carmen got me the phone number for the tour company that Square Café worked with on their coupon promotion. I was about to call them when I heard you and Carmen up front."

"Why not call them now?"

Meredith retrieved her phone from her pocket and swiped the screen a few times. "Okay, here it is."

She pressed the number and put the phone on speaker, then set it between them on the desk. After two rings, someone picked up.

"Travel Through Time Tours. What can we show you today?"

"My name is Meredith Bellefontaine. To whom am I speaking?"

There was a slight pause. "This is Abby. Look, if you've got an issue with a tour, we have an email address and an eight hundred number for complaints."

"No complaints," Meredith said. "Actually, I'm looking for someone to talk to about your coupon promotion. We were just at

Square Café yesterday, and the manager told us she had worked with you."

"Oh," Abby said brightly. "You'll have to speak to the manager. Let me see if she's in."

Abby put her on hold.

Julia looked over at Meredith. "What do you plan to ask her? I'm not sure what the connection is between Stephanie and the tour company, so I have no idea how to approach—"

"This is the manager," a woman said. "I understand you want to talk to us about a coupon partnership. What kind of business do you have?"

"Informational," Meredith said. "I guess you could say we are information gatherers. Anyway, could you please tell me how this works?"

The woman explained the process of arranging for the coupons and then having them printed. "We like print coupons. Some are going digital, but I find that the paper copies are better advertising. They tend to show up everywhere."

"How many drivers for your tours do you have?" Julia asked.

"Well," she said slowly, "right now we have about six. The number varies depending on the time of year. We find that August is a great month for tourists, but they only want the evening tours due to the heat."

"Who are your drivers?" Meredith asked.

"I'm sorry. What does that have to do with a coupon arrangement?"

"Nothing," Julia said. "We were just curious. As we said, we're in the information business."

"Right, okay," she said. "So I can email you the forms and you can complete them and return them along with your credit card number for the cost of the promotion."

"What if we want to pay in person? Can we do that?"

"Well," she said slowly, "we prefer to do things digitally."

"And I like to see the people I'm working with," Meredith said.

"Right, well, then are you familiar with where we're located?"

Julia read off the address from the website she'd pulled up while they were talking.

"Yes, that's correct. I'm here every day until five."

Meredith thanked her and hung up and returned the phone to her pocket. Julia turned her computer so Meredith could see.

"Look," Julia said. "They've got a page for photos. Let's see if we recognize anyone." She scrolled through to the end then sat back. "Nothing."

"I think I saw my hairdresser and her husband," Meredith said. "But I doubt she's involved in a dognapping."

"Probably not." Julia sighed. "Let's get back to Stephanie. I've bagged everything we took from her apartment." She reached for the first aid kit.

Julia opened the box and pulled the individual bags out to place them on her desk. "Nothing seems to be of much help—except, of course, for the pen with the ice cream connection."

Meredith shrugged. "At least we've got the bank deposit slip. I'll eat my hat if that doesn't mean something."

Chapter Eighteen

JULIA SUDDENLY THOUGHT OF SOMETHING she wanted to ask Amy, so she picked up her phone. "Amy," she said when the rings ceased. "I'm sorry to call during the morning rush, but can you spare me just a minute of your time? I've only got one question."

She could hear the sounds of people in the background, presumably her kitchen staff. "Sure, let me step outside for a sec so I can hear."

After a moment, Julia heard footsteps then a door opening and closing. The sound of birds chirping replaced the noise of clattering pans and voices.

"Okay," Amy said. "What's your question?"

"What time did Bosco get away from the dog walker?" Julia asked. "Specifically, I mean."

"I think it was around four."

"Okay, thanks."

"Hey, while I have you on the phone," Amy said, "did you happen to watch my interview on the morning show this morning?"

"I did. Meredith is here. I'm going to put you on speaker." She switched the phone to speaker mode and then placed it on the desk. "Okay, we're both on the line now."

"Awesome. So about the interview, I hope you didn't mind me giving Magnolia Investigations a shout-out. You weren't trying to remain a secret or anything, were you?"

"No," Meredith said. "It's fine. And by the way, I was watching too. I think what we were a little surprised by was the email and phone line for tips. If we're going to help you, we've got to stay informed, Amy."

"Oh, I guess I should have mentioned that. It happened kind of fast. Seth has been making things happen. I need to check and see if we've had any responses. I'll send you anything I get."

"That would be great," Julia said.

"Amy, I have a question for you," Meredith said. "Who thought of the hashtag and the whole cookie sale and…" She looked to Julia. "What else was it?"

"Expanded dinner hours," Julia supplied.

"Well, we had to send people away after word got out about Bosco. They were coming in to buy or to eat in, and I just didn't have the room to accommodate them. Selling the cookies online seemed like a good idea for getting my product out there without having to find space for the customers. And the dinner hours just sort of happened."

Julia and Meredith exchanged looks. "What charity are you going to give your cookie proceeds to?"

"We're still deciding, but it will be an animal shelter. Or shelters," Amy said.

"You and Seth? I assume he's a silent partner in your business," Julia said. "When I met with him yesterday, he was wearing a T-shirt with your logo on it."

Silence fell between them.

"Amy?"

"I'm here," she said meekly. "Look, I don't know much about all that. I'm a baker, not a business person. I let them handle that side of things for me."

"Who is 'them?'" Julia asked.

"Seth's people," she said. "But make no mistake, Julia. I own the building where the bistro is located. It's mine free and clear. Even if the bistro closed tomorrow, the building would still belong to me."

"Right," Meredith said. "You inherited it through a distant relative."

"My great-great-grandparents Oscar and Cora Bryant lived here. The building changed hands a number of times after they passed on, and their only child—my great-grandfather—didn't want it. A cousin of my father's found out it was for sale and purchased it but didn't do anything with it. When he died a year and a half ago, I was his only relative, so it went to me."

"I remember we were thrilled down at the historical society when we learned that you would be coming in and fixing it up to live in and run a business," Meredith said. "But back to the question I asked about the hashtag. Whose idea was all of that? You've certainly seen an uptick in sales, I understand."

"I guess I'm not sure why it matters."

Julia considered several responses. Finally she said, "We're just trying to get a clear picture of the situation so we don't miss any potential suspects."

"We want Bosco home again," Meredith said. "Hashtag or no hashtag. We're just a little concerned that it appears you might be profiting from this situation."

Silence again.

"I see," Amy finally said in a steely voice. "So you think I'm doing this to make money? Look, I would empty my cash drawer and my bank account to get Bosco back."

"But you haven't had to do that, because Seth is paying," Meredith said. "Amy, we know you love Bosco and want him home. But we have to ask the hard questions and eliminate all the possible scenarios until we figure out which is the correct one."

"I understand," she said.

"Just one more question," Julia said. "Would Kenton take Bosco and hide him so his and Seth's business could profit from a campaign to find the dog?"

"Why would he do that?" Amy asked.

"Because Kenton would do anything for Seth," Meredith said.

"No." Amy's voice broke. "He wouldn't take Bosco. I know he doesn't like me, but he just wouldn't."

"Amy," Meredith said again, "I'm sorry we've upset you, honey. I know you miss Bosco, and I hope all the things you're doing will bring him home sooner. Just remember to keep us in the loop."

"Thank you. I'll make sure." She paused. "There is just one more thing. It's so weird that I haven't told anyone."

"Amy, you can tell us anything—and I mean anything at all," Meredith said. "We won't think it's weird."

Julia gave her an incredulous look. Meredith shrugged.

"Sometimes I think I hear him."

Julia continued to hold Meredith's gaze. Then she shook her head.

"Hear him?" Meredith asked. "What do you mean?"

"Sometimes I hear Bosco barking. It sounds weird, I know."

"It sounds like you miss him very much," Meredith said.

"Well, yeah, but I literally hear him sometimes." She sighed. "Anyway, I'm probably just losing it."

"No," Julia said, "but it may be wishful thinking. You want to hear him, so you do."

"Okay," Meredith said. "Thank you, Amy. Good luck with the dinner service tonight."

"Thank you," she said. "I'm a little nervous, but I think we'll do okay."

"You'll do great," Meredith told her. "I'm sure Seth has a plan. Or Kenton does."

"Between the advertising and the…" She took a ragged breath. "Okay, if I keep talking I'm just going to make it look like they've done what you think they've done."

"What we suggested is possible," Julia corrected. "It's not our most likely theory, but it is a theory." Julia spied the AKC registration on her desk. "Do you possibly have one more minute for a question I've just thought of?"

"Sure."

"Who is S. E. Winter?"

"I don't know," Amy said. "I mean, Sooz Winter lives next door, but I have no idea what her middle name is. Why?"

"S. E. Winter is Bosco's registered owner."

"No she's not," Amy said.

"We've seen the AKC form," Julia said.

"You must have seen an old form then, because I'm Bosco's registered owner, not Sooz. I filled in the paperwork and sent in all the information to make that happen, so no one else's name should be on it," she insisted. "But I'll look into it, just to be sure."

"But Amy," Meredith said, "why didn't you mention to us earlier that you got Bosco from Sooz?"

"I guess I didn't think it was important," Amy said. "It's not like Sooz was reluctant to give him away. I had no reason to think she'd want him back." She sniffed, and Julia could hear the tears in her voice. "Besides, it's like I've always had him. I don't think of him being with anyone else but me, ever."

They said their goodbyes and then Julia hung up. "That was interesting."

"Good cop, bad cop strikes again," Meredith said.

"What do you make of her comment about hearing him barking sometimes?" Julia asked.

"Wishful thinking?" Meredith asked.

Julia shook her head. "Maybe. But what if it isn't? Bosco used to dig under the fence and go to Sooz's yard. Let's go see if we can speak to Sooz, and then we can find Stephanie Sterling."

Julia stood. "I'll drive. Just let me grab my keys, and we can go."

After determining that there were no parking spots nearby, Julia stopped in front of Sooz's to let Meredith out. She circled the block until Meredith reappeared on the sidewalk.

"Well that was interesting," Meredith said once she'd climbed in and buckled her seat belt.

"Did you talk to her?"

"I did indeed," Meredith said. "That Winter lady was not happy to see me. I asked her if I could look in her yard. It took some doing, but I finally convinced her. I'm sorry to say I didn't see any evidence of a dog there."

"Nothing?"

Meredith shook her head. "Not even a gnawed fence board or a hole big enough for a dog to wiggle through."

"Well, that is disappointing," Julia said. "I kind of hoped we'd find Bosco there and call it a day. Not that I've got any good reason to suspect her over any of the others on our list. But if Amy hears him…"

"If Amy hears him, then she must be imagining it," Meredith said.

A few minutes later, Julia typed the address for Pets Plus Warehouse into her GPS. Ten minutes after that, they pulled into a shopping center not far from Woof Walk.

The sign for the store dominated the middle of the shopping center. Julia parked in front, and Meredith followed her inside.

A glance around the store offered no visible sign of Stephanie Sterling. Julia walked over to the desk marked CUSTOMER SERVICE.

"Is the manager here?"

"Manager to Customer Service," the woman said over the sound system without responding to Julia directly.

"Thank you," Julia said sweetly. The woman merely nodded.

A few minutes later, an older man with graying hair and dressed in khakis and a polo shirt emerged from the back of the store. When he arrived at the customer service desk, the woman pointed to Julia without a word.

"How can I help you?" he asked.

"We understand you just hired Stephanie Sterling to work for you. I wonder if we could speak with her if she's here."

His brows rose. "And who are you exactly?"

Meredith handed him her card. "We just have a couple of questions to ask her. She's not in any trouble that we know of, so I hope this doesn't reflect on her employment status."

The manager hitched up his khakis. "She has no employment status until she finishes filling out the forms. That's the rule at corporate. I just enforce it." He shifted his gaze from Julia to Meredith then back to Julia. "I asked her to come a half hour early to get the papers completed, so she's not set to start until eleven. If you don't take up too much of her time, I'll allow it."

"Thank you," Julia said. "We won't keep her long."

He escorted them to the back of the store then into the hallway that led to the back of the building. He stopped at a closed door and inclined his head.

"In there. Remember, keep it brief, okay?"

Julia nodded. Meredith opened the door and stepped quickly inside with Julia following.

Stephanie's back was to the door as she leaned over a desk working on forms.

"I'm almost done," she said without looking up. "I just need to get my boyfriend's number off my phone for the contact information. I don't have it memorized."

"Stephanie?"

Her head shot up, and she turned around to face them. "Do you work here too?"

Julia went around the desk to take a seat. Meredith moved another chair around to the end of the desk then sat down.

"No," Meredith said. "We don't, but we are here about a pet."

Chapter Nineteen

"AMY BRYANT'S DOG, BOSCO," JULIA supplied as Meredith presented her business card to Stephanie. "We've been hired to find him, and we know you were the last person to see him before he disappeared last Friday."

Stephanie's eyes widened. "Look, that was an accident. I was walking Bosco, and he just got away."

"When you let go of the leash," Julia said. "That's the story we heard."

"Yes, that's exactly what happened."

"Again, we've heard that," Meredith said. "But there are some details I'm a little unclear about. You admit you let go of the leash, is that right?"

"Yes, I did," she said.

"Why, exactly, did you let go of the leash?" Meredith continued, taking her notepad out of her purse.

"It was an accident," she said. "Bosco pulled the leash out of my hand."

"And Bosco ran away," Julia supplied. "At Forsyth Park, possibly the most crowded public space in Savannah on an August Friday afternoon. And where no one the police questioned saw him."

Stephanie placed her pen on the table and sat back in her chair. "Wait. You guys aren't with the police, are you? Why should I talk to you?"

At Meredith's pointed look, Julia sighed. She would be the bad cop again. "You're right, Stephanie, we're not with the police. We just want to find Bosco, which I'm sure is what you want also. Unless, of course, I'm wrong about that, and you don't want him found."

Stephanie's shoulders sagged. "Look, I can't explain it any better than I already have. I wish it hadn't happened, but it did. Yes, I let go of the leash, but I don't know about whether anyone saw him."

Julia reached into her purse for her phone, pulled up the picture she'd taken at the apartment, and showed it to Stephanie.

"Is that your bank account?"

Stephanie's face paled. Then color rose in her cheeks.

"We found that in the apartment you vacated," Julia told her. "Who paid you to drop the leash, Stephanie?"

"And where is Bosco?" Meredith asked.

"I don't know where that dog is, and I promise that's the truth." She glanced down at Julia's phone then looked away.

"Then explain the bank deposit slip, please," Julia said. "I doubt your last job provided you with a five-thousand-dollar paycheck."

"I haven't done anything wrong."

"You also haven't told us who paid you," Meredith said.

"Why did you run away? Were you afraid?" Julia asked.

"I don't know. Maybe." Her shoulders slumped again.

"Of what?" Julia asked.

Stephanie looked up at her. "That's the problem. I don't know."

Meredith sighed. "Stephanie, help us help you. Someone told you to drop Bosco's leash last Friday. That same person must have told you when and where to be when you did that."

Julia nodded in agreement. "What we don't know is who reached out to you."

"Our job is to find Bosco," Meredith said. "The police have already said that this is not a matter they want to deal with. However, that could change."

"I was a lawyer and a judge for years," Julia told Stephanie. "In my experience, the courts tend to be much more lenient on those who cooperate. For your own sake, you need to tell us everything."

"Okay," Stephanie said. "I used to work at this tour company. I got fired. Back then I tended to oversleep, and sometimes I'd get on my phone when I shouldn't. I don't do that anymore, though. I promise."

"What's the name of the tour company?"

"Travel Through Time," she said. "Have you heard of it?"

"We have," Meredith said with a nod. "What does that have to do with the dropped leash?"

"I'm getting to it." Stephanie sighed. "So a couple of weeks ago my phone rings and it's from a number I don't recognize. Normally I wouldn't answer, and I never will again. I wish I hadn't then, because everything that's happened since then has been nothing but trouble."

"So your phone rang," Julia prompted. "Who was it?"

"Oh, I don't know. He never said. He said a guy at Travel Through Time gave him my number. He asked me if I wanted to make some extra money, and I said that depends on what I had to do. He said nothing bad. Just drop a leash at the time and place he tells me to and then walk away."

"That sounds pretty bad to me," Meredith said, scribbling away.

"I know it sounds bad, but he said it was because the dog's new owner wasn't good to it and he wanted to get it back so it'd be safe."

"So you thought you were helping Bosco?" Julia asked. At Stephanie's nod, she continued. "Did you ask him how he knew you worked at Travel Through Time and now at Woof Walk?"

"No," she said. "Anybody can go on Instagram or Facebook and see pics of me at work."

"You don't keep your sites private?" Julia asked.

She shook her head. "Nah. What's the fun in that?"

"So a man called and offered to give you money to drop the leash," Meredith said. "Did he give you all the details during that phone call?"

"No, he didn't. He said he would call when everything was arranged. I told him I wanted the money first, but he said we were doing things his way or not at all. So I said okay." She shrugged. "I needed the money, like really bad, but I also thought I was helping Bosco. I love animals. I would never ever hurt one. I just needed to drop the leash and keep my mouth shut. It seemed easy enough, and it would fix everything. Then he dropped off one of those burner phones under my mat at the apartment while I was at work. He told me to keep it with me and he would call with the time and date."

"Call, not text?" Julia asked.

"Yeah, no record that way." She shrugged again. "If he texted then there would be something to prove we arranged everything."

"How did he pay you?" Julia asked.

"Cash. Also under my doormat on the same day I dropped the leash. Well, actually he came in the middle of the night while I was sleeping." She paused. "His instructions were to put the phone under the mat, and he would pick it up and leave the money."

Julia leaned forward. "Did you see which direction Bosco went when you let go of his leash?"

Stephanie looked miserable. "I told everybody who asked he went toward the fountain, but that isn't what really happened."

"What really happened?" Meredith asked.

"I let go of the leash over at the tennis courts, by Court Four, like I was supposed to, and Bosco just sat there. He's a well-trained little guy, and he likes me. I knelt down and told him to run for it. When he didn't, I walked away."

Meredith looked up from her notes. "What happened then?"

"Bosco started following me. I kept walking toward the parking lot beside the tennis courts. That's where I was told to let go of the leash. Anyway, Bosco was behind me, but when I got to my car, he wasn't back there anymore. I guess the guy picked him up and put him in his car or something. If he hadn't gotten the dog, he wouldn't have paid me, right?"

"I wouldn't think so," Julia said. "So think hard, Stephanie. What did you do next?"

"I got in my car and drove back to Woof Walk to tell Mr. Duffy what happened. He got mad, and I kind of argued with him, so he fired me. After that, I went to my apartment, packed up, and took off. I was already late with the rent, so I didn't figure it would matter if I just left."

"Okay, just one more detail about the parking lot at the tennis courts. Think now," Meredith said. "Did you see anyone else in the lot, either in a vehicle or driving away?"

Stephanie looked as if she was concentrating on the question. Then she shook her head. "I can't remember."

"Try harder," Julia said. "Close your eyes and imagine the parking lot. Where was your car parked?" She told them, and Julia continued. "Okay, look around and tell me what you see."

"This is crazy," she said.

"Try," Julia said again.

"Okay, there were a bunch of cars and SUVs. There were some people playing tennis. That's all I remember. I was in a hurry to get out of there. Oh yeah, I was irritated because this big truck was blocking the exit. I had to wait for the dude to move."

"Tell us about this big truck," Meredith said, back to taking notes.

"I don't know. It was black with red letters on the side. Can't remember what it said, but I do remember there was something written on the back that seemed weird."

Julia shook her head. "What was that?"

Stephanie looked at Julia. "There was a phone number, which wasn't weird. But above the phone number it said 'Ring the Bell.' I mean, weird, huh?"

Bell. Julia picked up her phone and did a search for *Ring the Bell, Savannah.*

When the results popped up, Julia passed her phone to Meredith.

After glancing down at the screen, Meredith turned her attention back to Stephanie. "Did you see where the truck went when it moved for you?"

"I didn't really notice. I just wanted to get out of there," she said.

"Where have you been living since you left your apartment?" Julia asked.

"With my uncle Carl." Stephanie shifted her attention from Meredith to Julia. "You know Uncle Carl, right? I thought you looked familiar. He introduced me to you a couple of days ago."

"Yes, Meredith and I both know him. He delivers the mail to our office."

"He's a nice guy, but Ed acts a lot like a Fed sometimes even though she's retired. I guess she suspected that I had let go of the leash on purpose, and she told my uncle that." She paused. "After he got back from dinner with Ed, he asked a bunch of questions about what happened with Bosco. Then he said he needed to know whether I was involved in the dog going missing."

"Did you admit it to him?"

"No way. I didn't know if maybe he'd tell Ed and she'd call her buddies at the FBI and have me arrested or something, so I kept quiet."

"Stephanie," Julia said, "does the name Kenton Hollis mean anything to you?"

She shook her head. "Never heard of him."

"Seth Stevenson?"

"I only heard that name today when I was listening to an interview with Amy Bryant. It was either on the morning show or one of the radio stations on my way here. I can't remember. But she mentioned that Seth was her boyfriend and that she was worried about Bosco."

"Right." Julia paused. "What about a Dan Bell? Ever heard of him?"

Stephanie frowned. Then she shook her head. "Nope."

"You're sure?"

"Positive."

"Yet you hesitated," Meredith said.

"Yeah, I did. But that's because I was wondering if since the guy's last name is Bell he might have something to do with that weird message on the truck. Like maybe the phone number was his and the truck belonged to him. You know, like he's a trucker and he advertises?"

"Right." Meredith looked over at Julia. "Anything else?"

"Stephanie, are you sure you don't know where Bosco could be? Did the man give you any hint about where he might take him?"

"Just that he wanted him to be safe and that he wanted him back. Anything more than that, I didn't ask, and he didn't say. I was just thinking that I could really use the money, and I'm sure he wouldn't have wanted to answer anyway."

There was a knock at the door, and a moment later the manager opened it and stuck his head in.

"If you ladies are finished, I need Stephanie to get her paperwork together and come out on the sales floor to be trained."

"Just a few more minutes," Julia told him.

He nodded then raised his eyebrows at Stephanie. "Everything okay?"

"Fine," she said.

"Okay then." He closed the door.

Meredith consulted her notes. "Stephanie, is there anything else you'd like to tell us?"

"I hope when you find the dog you also find out who the guy was who got me into this mess." Stephanie clenched her fists. "I sure would like to tell him off."

"That's probably not a good idea," Meredith said. "Besides, you did agree, so the responsibility is on you, don't you think?"

She nodded. "Yeah. It's definitely on me. I won't make the same mistake again. I've learned my lesson."

When the door closed behind Stephanie, Julia let out a long breath. "Well," she said slowly, "that was an interesting interview."

Meredith nodded as she tucked her notepad and pen into her purse and rose. "And I predict the next one will be too. Let's go see Dan Bell."

Chapter Twenty

Savannah, Georgia
November 16, 1911

There he was again. Cora had seen Oscar at a distance a few times since their last conversation, but she'd always managed to slip away before he spied her.

Cora crossed to the other side of Abercorn Street to avoid seeing the man who was the talk of the neighborhood. She should have turned the other way at the park and missed Abercorn altogether, but she'd been in a hurry to get home from the market with a heavy bag before the skies did more than just threaten rain.

"Miss St. Germaine! Wait!"

Cora frowned. He'd seen her. Now what was she to do?

Though it was the last thing she wanted to do, Cora turned around. "Yes?"

Oscar—for she knew with complete certainty that he was not Oliver Clinton—caught up to her and smiled as he appeared to study her. An awkward silence fell between them. Overhead, the dark clouds continued to gather.

"Did you need something, Mr. Clinton?"

"Yes, sorry. I did." He shook his head. "Look, forgive me for staring, but you remind me of someone I knew briefly some years back."

Cora's breath froze in her lungs. She forced her expression to remain neutral.

"Unless she was from Savannah, it's unlikely it was me." The truth, and she managed to say it without clenching her jaw.

He held her gaze. "Honestly, I don't know where she was from, but I lost track of her and I've been trying to find her ever since."

"Why?" she uttered before she realized the word was out.

"I owe her something," he said. "And I miss her. But more than that, I just need to know what happened to her. She had such…" He paused long enough that Cora didn't think he would complete the sentence. "Spunk," he finally added. "She had spunk. And I think of her every time I make a stew. Every single time."

Tears sprang up just as the first fat drops of rain splattered around them. "I'm sorry, but I really must go."

"Wait, please. Let me get my umbrella and walk you home."

Cora shook her head and gathered her bag closer. "Thank you, but no."

She set off walking toward Oglethorpe Street, but Oscar fell into step beside her. Above them, lightning zigzagged across the sky. "I guess you've heard I'm opening a restaurant at the boardinghouse."

Cora answered with a nod then wiped the raindrops landing on her face. The sign for Oglethorpe Street was just ahead. She focused on it and not the man tagging along.

"I wonder if you'd consider coming to dinner. With me. At the restaurant. We're thinking of calling it Alma's since everyone here knows her and they don't know me. I guess I don't mind being the silent partner."

She focused on the Oglethorpe Street sign and picked up her pace. Home was getting closer with every step.

"You haven't answered," he said after a minute.

"I'm sorry, but I'm going to have to decline. Thank you all the same."

"It's because you don't know me," he said.

Hardly.

"I respect that," he continued. *"So may I call on you so we can get to know one another? Alma speaks very highly of you. And surely you value her opinion, given that it's your fault I found the building and Alma when I did."*

Cora stopped short and turned to face him. She was already soaked to the bone and the sky was spitting raindrops as thunder rolled, so avoiding the weather was no longer a reason to hurry home.

"Ty Cobb is starring in The College Widow *at the Savannah Theater tomorrow night. I could get tickets. I mean, who wouldn't want to see the world's greatest baseball player tread the boards along with another fellow you might have heard of, Billy Bolton? He's a star halfback, and Cobb, well, he's the Georgia Peach. They're not alone, mind you. There's apparently a cast of forty, or at least that's what the signs say."*

She'd read those signs. No one could miss them as they were plastered on every available space in Savannah.

"I'm sure my boarder Miss Havisham would love to go. She's the dramatic type and loves a good play. I doubt she knows the sports fellows, but then she probably won't care."

He wiped his wet face. "No offense to Miss Havisham, but I would rather you came along with me and not a stranger."

Cora shook her head. "But I am a stranger too, Mr. Clinton."

"Not to Alma, and she vouches for you." Oscar gave her a look that told her he thought the comment clever.

She sighed. "Look, I appreciate your kindness, and I am very happy for Alma. She's wanted to be more than a land-lady, and now she has the opening of this restaurant to look forward to. I'm sure you're a godsend in her eyes." Cora paused to shift the heavy bag to the other arm. "Please understand that while I am flattered you would ask to spend time with me, should you continue to do so, my answer will not change."

"I see," he said on a long breath. "Then since I can't warm up to it politely, I guess I'll just have to ask the question I've been wondering ever since I saw you at the door. It is why I am here in Savannah, actually."

Cora braced herself for the one question she never wanted to have to answer. Lightning flashed. Then from behind her came a loud boom. The ground beneath her feet shuddered, and she reached out to steady herself on a nearby fence.

Then came screams and the sound of someone yelling, "Fire!"

Chapter Twenty-One

AFTER THANKING THE MANAGER OF Pets Plus Warehouse for allowing them time with Stephanie, Meredith and Julia returned to Julia's car. "What did you think?" Meredith asked.

"I'm not sure." Julia turned the key in the ignition. "On the one hand she does seem like the naive type who might just want to help get a dog out of a bad situation. On the other hand, she freely admitted she needed the money. For me, that keeps me from fully believing she's that naive."

"I agree," Meredith said. "She seems sweet, but she let go of that leash for money."

"Big money," Julia said as she typed the address for Dan Bell's trucking company into the GPS. Just as she finished, her phone rang.

She dug the phone out of her purse and saw that it was Carmen. "What's up?" she asked.

"Carl was just here. He wanted to talk to you, but I told him that you and Meredith were out. He left his cell number and asked that you call him when you get a chance."

"Thanks, Carmen," Julia said. "Would you text me the number, please?"

"Definitely, but that's actually not the most interesting thing that's happened since you left."

"Oh?" Julia said.

"Yeah, there's a woman here demanding to see one or both of you. She's in the conference room with pimento cheese and crackers on a silver platter and refuses to leave until you talk to her."

Julia shook her head. "Who is she?"

"Suzy or Suzanne or something. She said it so fast I didn't get a chance to ask her which it was. Her last name is Winter."

"Sooz Winter," Julia said as Meredith looked up with a questioning expression. "Meredith and I just left her place not much over an hour ago. What could she possibly want with us?"

"Well, I don't know, but I can tell you that she stormed past me with her cheese and crackers and headed first into Meredith's office and then into yours. She was determined, I'll give her that, but she refused to believe you weren't at the office. Oh, and it was nice of her to cater the meeting she didn't have."

"Cater?"

"Yeah, like I said, cheese and crackers on a silver platter."

Julia started laughing then stopped herself. "I'm sorry, Carmen. It isn't funny."

"No it's not, unless you're the one not here dealing with her. When she settled into the conference room, I just left her there. Carl had to work around her to get the boxes out."

"Right, okay. So tell Mrs. Winter that Meredith and I will make an appointment to see her either this afternoon—not before three— or tomorrow. We're about to head to a possible interview and then maybe to a late lunch."

Julia turned in her seat to look at Meredith, and Meredith nodded in agreement.

"See, I tried that," Carmen said. "You know me. I'm good at managing people."

"That's one of the reasons we hired you," Julia said.

"Well, this one cannot be managed. I've been bested." She paused. "Great. I think I hear her snooping in the kitchen. I'd better go see. Just tell me one of you is coming back to the office to talk to her."

Julia held the phone away from her ear and gave Meredith a summary of the conversation. "I think we ought to handle the situation at the office first, don't you?"

Meredith sighed. "Tell her we're on our way."

"Did you hear that?" Julia asked.

"I did. Thank you."

"Just one more thing. Would you run her driver's license, please?" Julia spelled Sooz's full name. "Print off a copy so I can refer to it when we meet with her."

A few minutes later, Julia parked in her spot behind the agency.

Meredith unbuckled her seat belt. "Before we go in and deal with whatever Sooz Winter wants, let's talk about Stephanie's interview." At Julia's nod, Meredith continued. "Do you think we got the truth out of her?"

"I think we got some of the truth out of her. Maybe even most of the truth."

"What about how she ended up being contacted?"

"Okay, now that was interesting. This is the second time that particular tour agency has come up in this investigation. The Square Café, and now Amy. I think there's a connection that we need to investigate further."

"Right," Meredith said, "but remember both times it was in relation to Stephanie."

Julia nodded. "And as much as we're investigating the how of Bosco's theft, we were technically hired by Seth to figure out where Bosco is and return him."

"You find the how and you get the who," Meredith said. "But I agree. We need to be sure we're not getting off focus with our investigation."

"So we're agreed that we go check out Dan Bell after this to see if he's got the dog. If we believe what Stephanie said, he may be the person who hired her and picked up Bosco at the park."

"Emphasis on *may*," Meredith said. "Although I think her recollection of that truck was authentic."

"I think so too." Julia unbuckled her seat belt and reached for the door handle. "Let's go see what Sooz wants."

Meredith grinned. "And while we're at it, let's ask about her strange habit of giving Bosco collars that her nephew designs."

"We also need to find out who that nephew is, if we can," Julia said on a sigh. "I think that's important." Then she had a thought. "Meredith, we can't get so wrapped up in following the Dan Bell angle that we forget about Phillip Weber."

"Oh yeah, the lawsuit guy." Meredith reached behind her to retrieve her purse. "He's got an airtight alibi but definitely has a strong motive for revenge."

"He did file a lawsuit," Julia said, "but it could be argued that he's seeking his revenge through the court system. Although it could also be argued that the court system let him down when the sale of that card happened."

"Yes, true."

"And if Phillip Weber has the funds to sue, he may also be the money man who paid Dan Bell to do the actual snatching. Or they could be equal partners who both have it in for Seth and Amy."

"Agreed, except how did two random people who happen to have a mutual dislike of the same person find one another?" Meredith asked.

"Good question. It's a lot to consider," Julia said. "I sure wish I felt like we were closer to finding that dog."

"Well, we've certainly got a list of suspects."

Julia groaned. "And we can't forget the list Kenton Hollis sent us."

Meredith opened the kitchen door and found Sooz Winter standing at the refrigerator with Carmen watching from nearby.

"Sooz," Julia said, "why are you here?"

The woman straightened then turned toward Meredith and Julia and offered a smile. "Ladies, am I glad to see you. I was looking for something to drink that will go with the hors d'oeuvres I brought, but all you've got is water and Diet Dr Pepper."

"I told her that was all we have on hand today besides coffee, since I need to make a grocery store order," Carmen said. "And all of that goes just fine with pimento cheese and crackers."

Sooz straightened and gave Carmen a face that indicated she did not appreciate the comment. "My dear, that is hardly pimento cheese and crackers. I elevated the ingredients and created a whole new dish. It's not like I just slapped something on a plate and tossed some garnish on it."

The moment Sooz took her attention away from Carmen, Carmen shook her head.

"Let's go to the conference room." Julia looked over at Carmen. "Would you mind bringing me a Diet Dr Pepper? It was hot out there this morning, and I'm parched." She shifted her attention to Sooz. "What would you like?"

"Just water," she grumbled.

"Make that two, please," Meredith said as Julia led the way to the conference room.

With the boxes gone, the room was once again an elegant space to hold meetings. Just as Carmen predicted, there was a silver tray in the middle of the table that contained what looked like pimento cheese and crackers.

Rather than comment, Julia took a seat and indicated that Sooz should sit across from her. Meredith chose the chair at the end of the table.

After Carmen brought their drinks, she left and closed the door behind her. Julia regarded Sooz with curiosity, as much for the fact that the normally elegant woman looked a bit unkempt as for the idea that she'd been so insistent that they see her immediately.

"All right," Julia said to her. "We're here despite the fact that Meredith and I were called away from our errands and that you spoke with Meredith only a short while ago. What was so urgent that it couldn't wait?"

Sooz leaned in conspiratorially. "Something shady is going on next door, and I need you two to figure out what it is."

"Why didn't you mention this when I paid you a visit? Oh…" Meredith glanced at her watch and then back at Sooz. "Less than two hours ago?"

Sooz shrugged. "You were not expected," she said coolly. "Now that I've had time to think, I've got some things to talk about."

"All right," Julia said. "Like what?"

"For one thing, the tour buses are now stopping in front of her place. I mean, I do love the increased traffic on the street. My restaurant has received some attention from diners who don't want to wait in line at Amy's, so that's a plus."

Julia nodded and tried to keep a straight face. It was apparent that the only shenanigans going on were the result of Sooz Winter's jealousy at Amy's success.

"Yes, I would imagine it is," Julia said.

"But still, something is just not right there. I see delivery trucks all hours of the day and night." Sooz waved a cracker in the air for emphasis. "I run a respectable establishment, and everything was fine until that woman went and turned that old house into a bistro and bakery."

"That old house was crumbling until she moved in a year and a half ago," Meredith reminded her. "Restoration of the structure was a frequent topic at historical society meetings. So it's my opinion that Amy did the neighborhood a service—and also you, by the way—by taking an eyesore and making it something of value again."

Sooz shook her head. "That's a nice speech, Meredith. Spoken like the former historical society president I know you to be. However, neither of you happen to be Amy's neighbor, now do you?"

"We do not," Meredith said.

"Is this about the dog getting under your fence?" Julia asked. "Because that doesn't exactly constitute an emergency that would call us back to the office." She paused. "Unless he's back there now."

"Amy swears she's heard Bosco barking," Meredith added sweetly.

"Look," Sooz said, "I see you're not taking me seriously, and that's your choice. I just thought I might be helping. I went to the trouble of making a light snack because I thought we might be here until close to lunchtime, what with all I have to tell you. But if you want me to go, I will." She stood but made no move to retrieve her silver tray or leave the room.

"Sit down, Sooz," Julia said wearily. "Meredith and I are here, and we are willing to listen to whatever it is you've got to tell us. Just be specific. Generalities do not help."

"Okay, specifically there are trucks there at all hours of the day and night."

"Food delivery? Just like at your place?" Meredith asked.

"Maybe," Sooz said. "But what about the ones that come to the door when the bistro is closed?"

"Reporters and people who have heard about the missing dog and want to see the place for themselves?" Julia offered.

"Maybe." Sooz sat back in her chair and popped the cracker in her mouth. "But there are just things that aren't right there. You must look into her and her boyfriend and that business partner of his and, well, anyone else who associates with her. I mean, how in the world can someone as young as Seth Stevenson be so wealthy? And he's dressed in T-shirts and running clothes whenever I see him."

"And when are you seeing him?" Julia asked.

"Mostly when he's out in Amy's backyard. I can easily see it from several places in the upstairs storage areas. I just don't trust a wealthy man who doesn't look the part."

Meredith raised her eyebrows. Before she could respond, Julia nodded. "We'll do that, Sooz. Thank you for the tip."

"I'm just doing my civic duty," she said, obviously pleased with herself.

"Since you're here," Meredith said, "Julia and I have a couple of questions for you that we were eventually going to get around to asking about the case. Things you didn't give me time to ask earlier today." She paused. "If you're still willing to help, maybe you don't mind?"

"Go ahead," she said. "As long as you're taking my concerns seriously, I'll be happy to answer whatever questions you have."

Meredith smiled. "Do you have any family around here?"

Julia gave Meredith a look. Of all the questions to choose to begin with she had to go with that one?

"I do," Sooz said, "but I don't see what that has to do with the case. I prefer not to talk about it."

"You talked about it with Amy." At Sooz's confused look, Meredith continued. "She said your nephew designs pet collars. She allowed you to test them on Bosco."

"Oh yes," Sooz said reluctantly, "I guess that's true. But that's the extent of the conversation. My nephew is the private type. He wouldn't want me discussing his business with others."

"Or telling anyone who he is?" Meredith asked.

"Is he hiding something?" Julia asked.

"Oh heavens, no," Sooz said.

"I hoped not," Julia responded, "but I can't think of another reason why he would be so secretive."

"He just is," she said with a shrug. "Apparently he has business interests that require him to be circumspect. I'm always teasing him that he's a spy or with the CIA."

Meredith met Julia's gaze, her brows lifted. Julia elected not to comment.

"What was so special about those collars that required testing?" Julia asked. "It seems like a collar is a collar."

"He had different fabrics and thicknesses and all sorts of variables that he was working on to get it just right."

"And has he?" Meredith asked. "Gotten the collar just right?"

She seemed flustered. "I don't know."

"What kind of variables?" Julia asked.

Sooz shook her head. "Oh just different personalizations and things. Truly, I don't know all the options he's offering."

Meredith turned to Julia. "I'll just go get the papers from Carmen off your desk."

At Julia's affirmative nod, Meredith excused herself and stepped out of the conference room. "Where is she going?" Sooz demanded.

"Just to grab something she wants to show you." Julia picked up a cracker and dipped it into the pimento cheese mixture. "This smells delicious. Tell me what you've done to elevate the dish."

While Sooz waxed poetic on her culinary improvements to one of Savannah's beloved dishes, Julia helped herself to a second cracker. She had to admit it was good, but then she and Beau had never had a bad meal at Sooz's restaurant.

Meredith returned holding the AKC registration for Bosco and a copy of Sooz's driver's license. She placed the paper in front of Sooz. The woman's face paled.

"When were you going to mention that Amy's missing dog actually belongs to you?"

Chapter Twenty-Two

FOR A MOMENT, SOOZ SEEMED incapable of speaking. Then she recovered to offer first Meredith then Julia a smile.

"Yes, all right. Bosco was registered to me with the American Kennel Club when he was first purchased, but he belongs to Amy now."

"Amy says she sent in papers to make that change, but she didn't have any paperwork to show us that," Meredith countered. "I'm sure you understand why Julia and I are confused about this. Can you clear this up?"

"Well, of course." Sooz glanced out the window and seemed to be considering her words. "My nephew's friend had a litter of miniature schnauzer puppies that were available. This friend owed him a favor, so he got one of them for me."

"Okay," Meredith said. "That was nice of him, but how did Bosco end up with Amy?"

"He was a feisty little guy, as many puppies are, and I was busy running my business. I mean, a restaurant doesn't exactly run itself, and a puppy needs attention."

"So you offered him to Amy," Julia said.

"Sort of." She moved her attention from the courtyard outside the window to Julia and sighed. "Yes, that's what happened. I hate to admit that I gave him to her, because it seems disingenuous that I gave her the dog I later complained about."

"Perhaps a bit," Meredith said, taking a sip of her water.

"Bosco was going to be our test puppy for the collars. He turned out to be a handful, so he went to live with Amy not too long after she moved in next door."

"So a year and a half ago?" Meredith asked.

"Thereabouts, yes. He was just a puppy, but there was no way I could keep him." She shrugged. "He was much better off with Amy."

"But he kept coming to your backyard because it was familiar," Julia said.

Sooz nodded. "You understand, with our outdoor seating for the restaurant, we couldn't have a dog running around. The health department just wouldn't have it."

"I'm sure they wouldn't," Meredith said.

"So I had to be firm with Amy. Still, he was a cute little guy. And since we had the arrangement in place, it did make things simpler when he showed up, because I could just pop the next collar on him and send him home."

"When was the last time you did that?"

"Last Wednesday, maybe?" she said with a sweep of her hand. "Or was it Tuesday? I don't exactly recall."

There was a knock at the door, and Carmen stepped in. "There's someone to see you."

Julia exchanged glances with Meredith. Before either could speak, Sooz stood and collected her platter. "I'll just be going. I've taken up plenty of your time."

"We appreciate the information," Julia told her. "And we'll look into the things you've told us."

Sooz smiled. "Thank you for listening to my concerns. I would still love to see you and Beau at my restaurant soon." She turned to Meredith. "And you and whoever you're keeping company with. I promise I'll be more hospitable if I have some warning that you're coming."

"Thank you," Julia said before Meredith could respond. "We appreciate that, don't we, Meredith?"

At her partner's nod, Julia ushered Sooz from the room. Once in the center hall, she spied Carl speaking in low tones with Carmen.

Sooz brushed past without acknowledging Carmen or the mailman. Once their visitor was out the door, Julia smiled at Carl.

"Good to see you," she said. "And thank you for coming back to the office to speak to us. I'm sorry we missed you this morning."

"You were with Stephanie. She told me. That's why I wanted to see you as soon as possible."

Meredith stepped out of the conference room and waved a stack of papers at Carl. "Come on back, Carl. I'm just going to put these back in Julia's office and then I'll join you."

"Can we get you something to drink?" Julia offered as they walked down the hall past the coffee cart.

"Nothing for me," Carl said, "and I do appreciate you seeing me without an appointment. I know how busy you ladies are."

"No busier than you are," Meredith said when she arrived at the conference room door behind them. "Have a seat."

Carl settled in the same chair Sooz had just vacated. Unlike the restauranteur's cheerful bravado, he looked solemn and worried.

"What can we do for you?" Meredith asked Carl.

"It's what I can do for you." He turned his attention to Julia. "I should have told you about Stephanie when I saw you on the sidewalk outside that young woman's restaurant, Julia. It feels like I lied to you about something, and I don't like it. I owe you an apology."

"I did wonder why you didn't tell me her connection to the missing dog." She turned to Meredith. "We discussed Bosco's disappearance, though it was just briefly."

Carl sat back in his chair. "My sister passed away when Stephanie was a little girl, and my brother-in-law has had a time raising her. Stephanie is a good girl, but she's a bit unpredictable." He paused, his expression grave. "She finally admitted she got paid for letting go of Bosco. I told her if she didn't tell you, I would."

"She was very helpful when we spoke to her," Meredith said.

"She's afraid." He shrugged. "I guess she told you she's living with me now that she doesn't feel safe in that apartment."

"She did," Julia said.

"Well, yesterday afternoon I went over to the apartment just to check and see if she'd left anything of value that she would wish she had. There wasn't much there, actually, but I saw this poster of a music festival that I knew would mean something to her, so I grabbed that."

"I saw that on the wall beside her bed," Julia said. "The local festival at the riverfront from a few years ago."

"That's the one. It was my first year doing the festival, and she was so proud of me."

"Are you in a band, Carl?" Meredith asked.

"I'm a DJ." Carl grinned, his first since he arrived. "Carl 'DJ Fly' Flynt and the Fly Boys. We're all former Air Force guys, which is how we decided on the name. We do mostly eighties and nineties old-school hip-hop nights and weekends. The kids like it, and so do folks our age."

"I like it," Meredith said. "I had no idea you had this secret life as a famous DJ."

"I don't know about all that, but I enjoy it. It keeps me young." He shrugged. "Anyway, like I said, I knew Stephanie wouldn't want that poster to be thrown out, so I took it back to the car."

"Your expression tells me there's more to that story," Meredith said.

"There is," he said. "I know this is going to sound crazy, but I'm pretty sure I was followed."

"That doesn't surprise me," said Julia.

A look of relief washed over Carl's face. "So you believe me?"

"We both do," Meredith said. "Stephanie told us the man who convinced her to release her grip on Bosco's leash used the mat at her apartment's door as a drop-off point for a phone and then later a payment in cash. He knows where she was living and might have been watching to see if she returned, especially if he thinks she knows something."

"Did she tell you who this man is?" Julia asked.

He shook his head. "She claims she doesn't know."

Meredith frowned. "Can you describe the vehicle that was following you?"

"It was a black pickup truck. Late model. I believe it was a Dodge."

"Any distinguishing features that you noticed?" Julia asked. "A license plate number, a cattle guard, maybe some kind of customized grill?"

"Nothing like that," he said. "Just a plain black truck. The driver was wearing dark sunglasses and kept his visor down the whole time. I could make out a cap on his head, but that was about it. Most of the time the glare on the windshield kept him hidden."

"You're sure it was a male?" Julia asked.

"No," Carl said. "I'm just guessing based on the bulk of the driver and the fact that it was a truck. It could have been a woman, though not a slight one."

"Did you try to evade him?" Meredith asked.

"I made a few turns that I hadn't planned to make. I took a defensive driving class back when I was in the military. They said three left turns and you would know you were being followed if the same car was still behind you. So that's what I did. The driver was careful to never be right behind me, but he was there, make no mistake."

"So did you end up going home?"

Carl shook his head. "I went to work. I was off that day, but I parked behind a fence that's solid so folks on the street can't look in. The historical society did that for us as an improvement to the neighborhood—they painted some kind of scene of historic figures on three sides—and yesterday it was a godsend, I'll tell you." He paused. "I sat there for a while, and then I got out and walked to the street. When there was no sign of the truck, I drove home."

"Have you seen it since?"

"No, I haven't, so I'm hoping it was all just some kind of crazy coincidence." He met Julia's gaze. "Problem is, I'm having a hard time convincing myself of that."

Chapter Twenty-Three

JULIA LET OUT A LONG breath as she considered Carl's story. "I think you're right. You were definitely followed from Stephanie's apartment. The question is whether it was because someone recognized you or saw you leaving with something in your hand."

"Why would anyone want a poster I gave my niece several years ago?"

"I don't think they do," Meredith said. "But they may wonder if that was all you took from the apartment."

Understanding dawned on Carl's face. "So they may think there was something at that apartment worth having."

"Possibly," Julia said. "But I think it's more likely that they wanted to find Stephanie and thought they could through you."

He frowned. "Just tell me this. How much trouble is Stephanie in?"

"If Stephanie continues to be honest now that she's admitted she was paid to drop Bosco's leash, the amount of trouble she's in might be minimized," Julia said.

Carl exhaled sharply. "You don't know how relieved I am to hear that, Julia. I've been so worried about her. Like I said, she's flighty sometimes, but she's a good girl. I couldn't see her intentionally getting herself into trouble like that, but I can see her not realizing what she's agreeing to."

"Stephanie told us that Ed grilled her when she arrived at your place," Meredith said. "She likened your fiancée's questions to her work with the FBI."

Carl smiled again. "Ed worries about Stephanie as much as I do. With her mama gone, Ed has become a mother figure to her. So of course, given Ed's background with the feds, she's going to ask hard questions."

"Do you mind if we talk to Ed?" Meredith asked. "Not that we don't believe you or Stephanie, but sometimes another person will have a different perspective."

"No, that's fine," he said. "I want this dog found so we can get through the situation with Stephanie and have that behind her. She had a good first day at the pet store. But then she always was good with animals. That's why she kept that job with the dog walking service so long."

Meredith retrieved a slip of notepaper and pen from the sideboard and handed it to Carl then returned to her seat. "Would you mind giving us Ed's phone number and email address?"

He reached into his shirt pocket for his phone. "Ever since cell phones I've lost the ability to remember phone numbers. The convenience of just pushing a button next to a name has made my brain soft."

"I have the same problem," Meredith said. "If I ever lost my phone I couldn't call anyone." She paused to smile. "You're not alone in that."

"I'll let Ed know you'll be calling," he said. "She won't mind though. She'd do anything to help Stephanie get on track and stay there."

Carl handed the paper back to Meredith and placed the pen on the table. Then he stood.

"I've taken up enough of your time, ladies. Thank you."

"Just one more question," Julia said. "Have you ever heard Stephanie mention a man named Phil Weber?"

"No," he said.

"What about Dan Bell or Kenton Hollis?"

Meredith exchanged glances with her but said nothing. Julia returned her attention to Carl, who seemed to still be considering her question.

"No, I can't say as I have."

"Okay, well, let us know if you see that truck again," Meredith said. "And try to get a plate number."

"I will," he said, "but I'm hoping I don't see it."

They escorted Carl out of the conference room. When Meredith stepped out onto the porch with him, Julia stopped at Carmen's desk.

"Would you mind doing a rather extensive search for me?" Julia asked with a grin.

Carmen pulled up her search engine on her computer then reached for a pen and paper. "What do you need?"

"I need a list of all owners of black Dodge pickup trucks in this city." She shook her head. "No, let's make it Chatham County. We're looking for a late model, so let's say 2017 to 2021. We can revisit if we need to, but I think that's a good range. And yes, I know that's going to be a long list."

"Okay," Carmen said as she took notes. "Anything else?"

"Yes, see what you can find out about a company that makes dog collars locally. I don't know anything about a name for it, but check to see if Sooz Winter might be associated with it, please. It's a long shot, because she says her nephew is designing the collars, so she might not be included, and he might not be incorporated or even have a business name."

Carmen wrote something down and then looked back up at Julia. "Check."

"Oh, and while you're checking, please see if you can get me a list of the corporate entities owned by Kenton Hollis."

"Seth's best friend?" Carmen shook her head. "Why?"

"I just wonder what other ventures he's involved with that might benefit from Bosco's disappearance."

"So another search just like we'd do for a client."

"Exactly," she said. "And please don't mention this to Amy."

"Okay, sure."

Julia smiled. "Just one more thing. Have you heard anything from the tip line that Amy—or whoever—set up?"

"*Nada*," Carmen said. "I actually talked to Amy about that while you were in the conference room with Carl. I figured you'd be asking. She said there were a bunch of calls but they were all sounding pretty fake. Seth has a team going over them."

"Interesting that he has a team since he hired us," Julia said.

Carmen nodded. "Right? I told her the same thing."

Meredith came back inside. "I sat in the swing until Carl left. He told me he was parked around the corner, so I asked him to drive past the office on his way out. I wanted to see if a black truck was following him."

"And?"

She shrugged. "Nothing. Carl may be right in thinking that whoever it was figured he was of no interest to him."

Julia sighed and then said, "Well, I think we need to talk about what just happened in the conference room."

"With Sooz or Carl?" Meredith asked.

"Both," she said. "But we also need to track down Dan Bell. How about we compare notes over lunch and then go find our high school bully turned truck driver?"

"Yes, let's," Meredith said. "We're overdue for the Downhome Diner. Let's go there." She paused. "And Carmen, can I add one more thing to your workload?"

Carmen made a face then laughed. "Of course. What is it?"

"Would you get us an appointment with Seth? Tomorrow if possible, and I want him to come here. We need to see Amy's boyfriend on our turf, not his."

Julia slid her a sideways look. "I'm guessing you'll tell me what this is about over lunch."

"Absolutely." She grinned at Carmen. "You are a treasure. Thank you."

"You know even a treasure has to eat," Carmen called as they walked down the hall toward the back door.

"Order something for yourself and have it delivered," Julia said with a chuckle. "Charge it to the office."

"*Gracias*," drifted down the hallway and chased them out into the August sunshine.

***

"I always forget how hot it gets in August until it is August," Julia said as she stepped into the air-conditioned coolness of the Downhome Diner.

One of their favorite dining spots in Savannah, the Downhome Diner was owned by Charlene Jackson, daughter of their dear friend Maggie Lu King. With cheery yellow walls and a sparkling counter with red vinyl-covered stools, the diner exuded retro charm.

Despite the time being well past the normal lunch hour, the diner was doing a brisk business. Justine, one of their favorite waitresses at the diner, ushered them to a table near the window overlooking the street and left two menus and two glasses of water with them. A few minutes later she returned to take their orders.

"Brunswick stew and a Diet Dr Pepper for me," Julia said.

Meredith handed the menu back to Justine. "Today I think I'll have the chicken salad sandwich." She looked down at the waters on the table then back up. "Water is fine."

"Is Charlene here?" Julia asked.

Justine smiled. "No, she's with Clarissa today."

Charlene's daughter, Clarissa, was the mother of an adorable baby boy named Jake. Each time Meredith and Julia dined at the Downhome, they were treated to new pictures.

"Playing with that grandbaby," Meredith said. "I understand that."

"Mrs. King is here though," she said. "I think she's working on something for Charlene in her office."

"Maggie Lu is here?" Julia exclaimed. "Would you please tell her we're out here? We don't want to disturb her if she's busy, but we would love to say hello if she has a moment."

"Yes ma'am. And I'll get these orders in," Justine said as she departed.

Julia retrieved her notebook and pen. "Okay, until Maggie Lu joins us—if she does—let's talk about the case. What is this about an appointment with Seth? And why on our turf?"

Meredith took a sip of water. "Seth bought a special dog collar for Bosco and had it sent to Amy."

"Yes," Julia agreed.

Meredith paused as if considering her words. "So why a dog collar? Wasn't that poor dog already subjected to enough new collars, all the time?"

"Well, not all the time, but it does sound like there were frequent changes," Julia said.

"So of all things, Seth—who we know is prone to giving Amy extravagant gifts—sends her a dog collar, knowing that Bosco gets free collars from next door." She shook her head. "Why?"

"Good question." Julia made a note about that in her notebook then looked back up at Meredith. "I have no answer for that. It doesn't make sense, does it?"

"Not at all."

"And Bosco went missing the same day the new collar was put on him." Julia paused. "What's the connection?"

"I don't know," Meredith said.

Justine returned with their meals. Julia was about to dig in to her Brunswick stew when she saw Maggie Lu emerge from the office. She and Meredith met her halfway and exchanged hugs then led her back to their table.

Maggie Lu King was tall and regal with hair that refused to go completely gray. Her smile was broad, and her eyes sparkled.

"Thank you for joining us," Meredith said. "What a nice surprise."

"Well, you two are a nice surprise indeed. Charlene is looking to make some improvements to her office back there, so I offered to take on the challenge of wallpapering. It's beautiful, but goodness, do not ask me to do it again for a while."

Julia laughed with her. "I tried to paper a bathroom right after we moved to the house in Live Oak. Three days in, Beau put a stop to it and hired someone. It saved our marriage, I'll attest to that."

"I just hire that out," Meredith said. "I've never liked anything that required exact measurements and sticky glue. You are a brave woman, Maggie Lu."

"When I was younger, I loved to do things like this, but I am decidedly feeling my age. Now go on and eat." She motioned to Justine. "I have earned an iced tea and a break."

She ordered her tea, which Justine brought with all the speed expected when serving an honored customer. "So what's new with my favorite private detectives?" Maggie Lu asked. "Or can you tell me?"

"We're looking for a lost dog."

"That missing pup that belongs to the Bryant girl?" Maggie Lu took a sip of tea.

"That's the one."

"Oh, he's a cute little fellow. Charlene ordered little dog-shaped cookies from that bakery to sell here. They're all gone now, so they must have been tasty."

"He is cute," Meredith said. "We're doing our best to bring him home, but the case is a little more complicated than we expected."

"Doesn't that generally seem to be the way with you two?" Maggie Lu asked. "I was certainly glad to see Amy make something of that old house she inherited. I wonder if she knows about its history."

Meredith recited what she knew about the building from her work at the historical society. Maggie Lu listened and nodded.

"Yes, all of that is true, but there's more to that story." She paused to take another sip of tea but held the glass in front of her rather than return it to the table. "It was built as a home way back sometime in the 1800s."

"I believe it was 1864," Meredith interjected.

"Yes, that sounds about right." Maggie Lu set her tea glass on the table. "The owners were Unionists and German, so they were untouched during the war, except perhaps for the disdain of their neighbors, or so the story goes. Once the war was over, they took off to Germany. The house was sold and divided up to become a boardinghouse. It stayed that way well until the early 1910s. But that's where things really get interesting."

Chapter Twenty-Four

The boardinghouse that Alma had set her dreams on now lay in smoldering ruins. Once the lightning struck, it had taken little time for flames to spread from the attic throughout the old building.

The fire brigade was gone now, and blackened posts where the grand front porch had been stood sentry over a home where only the fireplaces remained. There were four of them—two in the front and two in the back—and their brick silhouettes jutted up into the clearing skies.

Dazed boarders stood in clusters on the sidewalk with blankets draped over their shoulders while Alma paced and wrung her hands. Oscar was seated on the back of a cart, allowing a doctor to bind his arm. Neighbors milled about, some mixing with the boarders and others watching from behind the safety of their iron fences or, in some cases, their heavy drapes.

As if to add insult to injury, sunshine pushed the remainder of the clouds away and cast the scene in a bright yellow glow. The sidewalk in front of Cora shimmered even as she shivered.

Ida caught up to her, a basket tucked into the crook of her arm. "I thought some of those meat pies we planned to serve the boarders would be best used with those who don't have a table to sit at tonight."

"Good idea," Cora said. "I'm sure our people won't mind if they give up their meal. We've got bread and leftover ham for sandwiches. That'll do for the ones who complain."

"And for the ones who don't," Ida added evenly. "I aired out the extra mattresses and put as many as I could where I could fit them, so with your permission I'm going to spread the word that we've got room for a few to stay until they can get themselves situated elsewhere."

Cora's eyes remained on the awful scene unfolding in front of her. "Yes of course," she said.

Ida sighed. "Right now those are the people who need some encouraging. All I've got to offer them is this basket of pies, but I think it'll do for now. There's more baking to be done, so I'll need to be quick about this."

She left Cora's side and marched into the fray, handing out food to anyone who indicated an interest. Cora remained rooted in place. What did she have to offer?

Then from nowhere a song rose up inside her. A hymn of praise. Of hope.

Since she'd left Carnegie Hall to step into Oscar Bryant's kitchen, Cora had never once sung alone in public. With the choir at practices and on Sunday morning, certainly. But *even then she'd kept her voice subdued and let others take the spotlight.*

Oscar met her gaze and offered a nod in greeting. Cora lifted her hand to respond.

Ida's words came to mind. "When it happens, you won't be able to stop it. And it's going to bring comfort and hope to someone. Mark my words."

Cora's gaze swept across the scene. Heads were bowed, voices quiet, eyes downcast. Behind them the charred wreck of their lives still smoldered.

She took a few steps forward. There must be something else she could do. Something else that would be helpful. Something else to give her neighbors hope.

Just as Ida promised, the song rose, and Cora was unable to hold back the words. She closed her eyes, knowing well what might happen if she revealed this voice—the voice that was meant to praise God—as belonging to her.

There would be no more hiding.

Cora inhaled deeply and let the breath out slowly. Yes, it was time.

"'When peace like a river attendeth my way. When sorrows like sea billows roll.'"

Her voice echoed in the quiet air, at first tentative and then growing stronger as she found her courage. Though her eyes were still closed, Cora felt the attention of those around her shift. Then gradually a chorus of friends and neighbors joined in.

"'It is well, it is well, with my soul,'" she finished as the people around her applauded.

Cora opened her eyes to see Oscar Bryant standing before her. A single tear traced its way down a face smeared with ashes and soot.

Ida approached with a look on her face that seemed to say I told you so. "Preacher will be here soon, and you know how he likes my cooking. I'm going to go check on that next batch of pies."

"All right," Cora said.

"Coraline," Oscar whispered when Ida was gone.

"Just Cora now, please," she managed. "I'm just Cora. Nothing special anymore, and I like it that way."

He wiped his cheeks then looked down at his hands. Finally his gaze rose to hers again. "You'll never be just Cora to me, and you will always be something special."

She mustered a smile though her knees were threatening to buckle. "Oscar Bryant, you owe me a recipe for stew."

"I owe you more than that." Oscar laughed then quickly sobered. "There are things about me you don't know. You're not the only one who's been hiding from the past."

"I assumed that when you announced yourself as Oliver Clinton."

Oscar shrugged. "I wasn't sure it was you. I didn't expect you to be running a boardinghouse, though it suits you." He tapped his temple. "That recipe is up here, so I would have to show you."

Cora smiled. "I would like that. And perhaps another cake?"

"With extra cardamom," he told her. "First I have to make a trip to Atlanta to handle some business I should have resolved a long time ago. I can't say how long it will take, but it might be a while. However long I'm gone, I'll be back, and when I return I'll explain everything. Just know that wherever you are, I'll find you. I promise."

❧ Chapter Twenty-Five ❧

"You tell the best stories, Maggie Lu," Meredith said. "I wish you'd come speak at one of the historical society meetings."

Maggie Lu waved away the statement. "I just pass down what I've been told to keep the stories alive. I might take you up on that sometime, but for now I enjoy talking to you two."

"So what happened in the 1910s?" Julia asked.

"Oh, that is such an interesting story. My Granny Luv was a young woman then and had a friend, Miss Ida Allen. Miss Ida—she never did marry—was lady's maid to the St. Germaine family back when folks did that sort of thing. She never would say how the turn of events happened, but Miss Ida, she ended up working at this very boardinghouse we're talking about. That'd be around 1905 or 1906, though I might be off on that date by a bit."

"I'm sure not by much," Meredith said with a smile. "I'd pretty much take your memory to the bank."

Maggie Lu smiled back at her. "The owner of the boardinghouse was Cora St. Germaine. She and her mother up and left Savannah one day and no one heard a peep from them until years later Cora suddenly showed back up one day. No one but Miss Ida knew where she'd been—only that her mama had passed away—and neither she nor Miss Ida was telling. Eventually people stopped asking."

She paused as Justine stopped by the table to check on them. Though she tried, she couldn't convince Maggie Lu to order anything.

"You tell my daughter I'm eating just fine and she needs to stop calling to check on me," Maggie Lu said with a chuckle. "That Charlene fusses over me, but much as I complain, I have learned to like it."

She shook her head. "Anyhow, where was I? Oh yes, a few years later there was a fire at another boardinghouse around the corner that sent all the folks out to the sidewalk, scrambling for their lives. Miss Ida and Cora, they took in all who could fit. The way Granny Luv told it, there were folks sleeping under the attic rafters that night, but that's not the most interesting part." Maggie Lu paused.

"Don't stop now," Julia said. "You've got me hooked. What happened next?"

Maggie Lu shook her finger at her. "I'm getting ahead of myself. You see, Cora had always been a quiet child. Miss Ida told Granny Luv it was all her mama could do to get her to sing in the church choir, but she blossomed there and even sang a solo or two. And that day when the fire took that house, well, I'm told she stood on the sidewalk and sang like an angel." Maggie Lu shook her head. "A real live angel is how Granny Luv told it."

"How beautiful," Julia said, imagining the scene.

"I'm told it was. But there's even more to the story than that." Her eyes glistened. "The man who owned the building that burned hadn't owned it long. Miss Ida said he'd come to Savannah looking for his long-lost love, but he couldn't find her." She paused again. "It had been years, but when he heard that song, he knew the sound of her voice."

"I'm getting chills," Meredith said. "What happened then?"

"She walked right into his arms," she said. "So Amy Bryant is here because of a house fire and a woman who listened to the Lord and sang to hurting folks. Now that doesn't mean there wasn't trouble that nearly kept them apart again, though Miss Ida didn't want to talk about that except to say it was a Christmas miracle that saved it all." She breathed deeply and then said, "Isn't it something how the Lord works?"

"It is," Julia whispered. "What a beautiful story. Does Amy know about this?"

"I've not spoken to her, so I wouldn't know, but she ought to." Maggie Lu shook her head. "Goodness, I've taken up all of the conversation."

"I've enjoyed every minute of it," Meredith said as Julia nodded.

"Well, be that as it may, it's nearly two o'clock in the afternoon, so you either had a late start or a busy morning. In either case, I'm guessing you've got a busy afternoon ahead of you, and I have a few things to attend to myself later on."

"Just one interview," Julia said. "We're hoping it will give us the clue we need to find the dog."

"Well, amen to that," Maggie Lu said. "Now how about you two finish your lunch. I'd rather hear about what's going on with you anyway. Before you leave, we'll pray about that poor girl who's missing her pup, and we will ask the Lord to lead you right to him."

"We can do that," Meredith said, and Julia nodded in agreement. "And maybe you'll consider speaking to Amy about her history once this case is wrapped up."

"Why don't I just write it all down for her?"

"That would be wonderful, Maggie Lu," Julia said. "I'm sure she would be thrilled."

After lunch the ladies decided to return to the office to regroup and do a bit more research on Bell. Then they started off toward the address Julia had put into the GPS earlier that day. The house was in an older and less fashionable part of Savannah.

Adjacent to the front door stood a black lamp pole with a small gas flame that probably lit the front porch. A heart-shaped sign dangled from beneath the street-side mailbox. On the sign was a 1980s-era duck wearing a Wedgwood-blue bow from which a mauve heart dangled. Beneath the duck the names GRANDMA AND GRANDPA BELL had been written in block letters.

Dan Bell went to high school with Seth, thus he was not likely to be Grandpa Bell. Had Kenton or Seth told her that Dan was living in his grandparents' home? She would have to check her notes, but that appeared to be the case.

Julia parked the car and snapped a few photographs. "I don't see a truck like the one Stephanie described here. Should we just sit tight and hope one shows up?"

"Or a black Dodge pickup," Julia said. "And maybe so."

Julia grabbed her phone to check her emails. She was scrolling through the list when Meredith nudged her.

"Look at that," she said. "It appears Dan Bell just came home."

A truck fitting the description Stephanie gave them slowed to turn in to the driveway of the home. The driver turned off the engine but remained in the car.

"Do you think he saw us?" Meredith asked.

"How would he recognize us?" Julia asked. "Neither of us have met him."

"Right." She nodded. "Of course."

A few minutes later, a man wearing navy-blue work coveralls climbed out of the truck and stuck a hat on his head. He was tall but not overly so and built like a linebacker. He took a few steps toward the front door then stalled and turned around.

"Now I know he's seen us," Meredith said.

"No, look. He just forgot something." They watched as he reached into the truck and retrieved a cell phone then tucked it into his pocket.

Julia opened the car door and closed it softly then headed toward him before she changed her mind. "Mr. Bell?" she called.

The man swiveled and stopped. "Yeah, who's asking?"

"Julia Foley," she said, producing a card and thrusting it toward him. "And that's my partner Meredith Bellefontaine."

At least she hoped Meredith was behind her. She didn't want to take her attention away from Dan Bell to check.

Bell looked down at the card but made no move to take it. "What do you want? The truck's hired out for the rest of the week, but I've got some time on Saturday afternoon. Otherwise it'll be Tuesday before I can do a pickup or delivery for you."

"Actually we don't want to hire out your truck," Meredith said. "We've just got some questions for you."

He looked down at Julia's card. "You're cops."

"We're not," Meredith said before Julia could. "We work for Seth Stevenson. He wants Bosco back."

Bell's eyes narrowed. "Yeah, well, tell Pee Wee Stevenson that I don't have his little girlie dog."

"Don't have it," Julia said, "or don't have it anymore? Because we have a witness who says that your truck was in the parking lot by the tennis courts at Forsyth Park on Friday afternoon at four o'clock, where the dog was last seen."

"We figure if you don't have him then maybe you passed him off to someone else. Do you haul just anything in your truck, Mr. Bell?" Meredith asked. "Because I'm sure a miniature schnauzer would fit."

Bell shook his head as he waved away Meredith's comment. "If it was April Fool's Day you two would be hilarious. Since it's not, get off my property and tell Seth Stevenson to leave me alone."

"Seth doesn't know we're here," Julia said. "We're just doing our job as investigators by following the trail of evidence."

"Well, the trail stops somewhere else, because it doesn't stop here." He walked toward the door then paused. "You're trespassing. Get off my property, or I'll call the real cops."

He went inside and slammed the door but soon reappeared at a window overlooking the porch. He lifted his cell phone into view and pointed to it.

"We should go," Julia said. "He's right. We could be considered trespassers."

They returned to Julia's car but not before Julia sent a picture of the truck and the license plate to Carmen. CHECK THIS NUMBER OUT, PLEASE, she texted.

Then she called Wally. "I've got a quick favor to ask. If I give you a name and an address, would you tell me if he has any priors or warrants?"

"Absolutely," he said. "What's the information?"

Julia told him.

"Hang on a sec." Wally put her on hold but came back quickly. "He's clean."

"Okay." She let out a breath she hadn't realized she'd been holding.

"You sound disappointed. Was this guy someone you've been looking for?"

She opened the driver's door. "I'm not sure. Thanks, Wally."

Meredith held up her phone. "Carmen texted us both on this one. We've got a meeting with Seth tomorrow morning at nine."

Julia's phone dinged twice. She looked at her texts and saw that one was the appointment reminder with Seth. The other one, also from Carmen, was longer.

PLATE COMES BACK DANIEL WILSON BELL. DID CHECK ON HIM. HE'S 97 WITH A LICENSE SUSPENDED DUE TO AGE INFIRMITY. GRANDPA ALSO OWNS THE BUSINESS ASSOCIATED WITH THE NAME ON THE TRUCK.

Julia read the text to Meredith.

"Okay, so Dan is driving Grandpa's truck and has taken over his business," she said. "Meanwhile his old nemesis is a millionaire a few times over. That can't sit well with someone who used to be a bully."

"He called Seth 'Pee Wee,' so I'm guessing he's still a bully," Julia said.

"If he's involved, it probably didn't take much to convince him to put Bosco in his truck and drive away."

"I wish we had a video...." Julia paused. "Of course. The tennis courts are near the edge of the park right on the street. There's just a parking lot and some trees between the courts and the road."

"And there are stores across the street. Oh Julia, of course. Someone may have caught it on video."

Meredith dialed Carmen's number and put her on speaker-phone. "*Hola*," Carmen said when she answered. "Let me guess. You have another search for me."

"Not exactly," Meredith said. "We just need you to call the businesses that face the tennis courts at Forsyth Park and see if anyone has video footage from around 3:45 to 4:30 last Friday afternoon."

"And I should drop the other things and do that now?"

"Please," they said in unison.

"And thank you," Meredith added.

"I better have a good Christmas bonus this year," Carmen joked.

"We promise," Julia said. "Let us know if you come up with anything."

"On which assignment?"

"On any of them, but specifically the camera," Meredith said. "And if you run out of things to do…"

"La-la-la," Carmen sang. "I'm hanging up now."

"Bye, Carmen," Meredith called, "and thank you."

Julia buckled her seat belt and leaned back against the seat, contemplating the events of the afternoon. Then she looked at the clock.

"It's almost four," she said. "Let's head back to the office then walk over to the tennis courts. I'd like to walk through the scenario that Stephanie described to us."

Once they reached the office, Julia and Meredith dashed inside and dropped their purses in their respective offices, then walked up to the reception area.

"Something else you need me to do?" Carmen asked.

"We appreciate you," Julia told her. "And we've kept you busy today. If you've finished making the calls to the businesses, then why don't you go on home?"

Meredith nodded. "I'll have the calls routed to my cell and that way we won't miss anything."

"Yeah?" Carmen asked.

"Yeah," Meredith responded as Julia nodded in agreement.

"Okay, well, I've got a list here of all the businesses facing Park Street. I've placed calls to all of them. Since our office is just around the square from them, every manager was cooperative. However, not one of them keeps their security film on site. That's the bad news. The good news is, of the seven businesses, there are only two security companies represented. I'm just waiting for calls back right now, though I'm not sure whether I'll hear from the managers or the security companies." She stood and smiled. "I'll just get my leftovers and go home. Thank you for the extra hour of free time today and for the delicious lunch you paid for."

Carmen hurried off. The refrigerator door opened and closed and then the same happened with the back door.

When Julia heard the click of the lock at the back door, she nodded toward the front door. "Time to head to the park."

They walked past the azaleas and onto the trail that entered Forsyth Park on the diagonal. At the center of the park, the ladies turned left toward the tennis courts at the far end of the green space.

Finally they reached the spot where Stephanie described letting the leash go. "Okay," Julia said. "We're here. She said she dropped the leash, but the dog didn't go anywhere."

Meredith shook her head. "So next Stephanie said she walked toward her car, which was parked over there." She pointed to the parking lot between the tennis courts and Park Street. "So she was somewhere over there."

Julia started walking that way. "Since all the spaces are to the left of the sidewalk that runs past the courts, she would have had to turn in that direction. The truck that was blocking her would have either been here by this end of the courts or down there at the other end."

"Either way, I can see how it all went down as she said."

Julia stopped to survey the lot. "And depending on which way Bell went, the cameras at the stores—if there are any—would have caught an image of him."

"And hopefully an image of a fuzzy little passenger."

As they retraced their steps back to the office, Meredith sighed. "I don't know about you, but I'm ready to call it a day."

Julia agreed. "I just want to go home, put my feet up, and not move for a couple of hours."

Meredith stopped suddenly. "I think you're going to have to put that plan on hold, Julia."

Julia followed her line of sight and groaned. Two figures were sitting on Magnolia Investigation's front porch swing, and she knew at least one of them was used to getting his way.

Seth Stevenson.

ᨠ ᨠ Chapter Twenty-Six ᨠᨠ

More than a year had passed since Oscar had left Savannah and Cora. She'd sent a dozen letters to the Trask Detective Agency in search of him, but thus far there was no trace.

Cora had been tempted to travel to Atlanta herself and comb the city until she found him. He'd promised to return but hadn't told her how long it would take.

She adjusted the combs she'd put in her hair for tonight's performance then stepped back from the parlor's pier glass mirror. Under any other circumstances, Cora wouldn't have tried to call attention to herself like this. After her years on the stage as the center of attention, she rather liked being anonymous. Invisible.

But she hadn't been invisible to Oscar. He'd seen her then, and he'd seen her last year when they were reunited.

And he'd promised to return.

"You'd best hurry up," Ida told her as she hurried through the parlor on her way to the kitchen. "We'll be feeding a

houseful for sure after church, so there's no time for standing around and looking at how beautiful you are."

Cora shook her head. "I assure you that is the last thing I see when I look in the mirror."

Ida stopped short and turned around. "Well, it ought not to be," she said. "Don't you think it's about time you see yourself as everyone else does?"

Cora waved away Ida's words with a sweep of her hand.

"You might ignore me, but that doesn't make it any less true. Now get on over to the church. They'll likely want to practice a few times before it starts. I'll be here to greet everyone when it's done."

"It's Christmas Eve, Ida. Surely you don't intend to miss church."

"Didn't say I would," she stated matter-of-factly. "But I plan to be seated by the door so I can get out and run home. I've got to greet the callers, and you know how Miss Bessie and her sister like to leave as soon as the plate is passed. Surely they will be standing on the porch waiting no matter how early I slip out."

"I'm grateful for you," Cora told Ida. "I don't know what I would do without you."

It was Ida's turn to dismiss the words. "You'd do just fine, and I won't hear anything more about it. That new preacher was right in insisting you do the honors this year. I wasn't sure how I would like Reverend Sanders, but I've decided he's going to fit in here just fine."

Cora mustered a smile that fell as soon as Ida left the room. She took a moment to glance around the parlor, which had been decorated to perfection by Ida with a combination of Mama's Christmas decorations and greenery collected from the local florist. The Christmas tree stood in the corner, its candles ready to be lit as soon as the guests arrived. Cora blew out a long breath, gathered her wrap, and hurried off to church.

True to Ida's prediction, there were several opportunities to practice the music that had been chosen for the evening, and Cora flubbed every single one. Since her foray into singing solo back on the day of the fire, she had been prodded to repeat the performance in services at Wesley Methodist Church on Sunday mornings. For more than a year she had successfully declined in favor of others who willingly stepped forward to perform. Until tonight.

She sighed. What in the world was Reverend Sanders thinking when he insisted she be the soloist?

"Shall we try it again from the top, Miss St. Germaine?" the choral director asked, her voice high and nasally and her disapproval evident.

"No time for that," the preacher said as he stepped into the room. "Come, let's go in and worship, shall we? It is indeed a night divine."

His gaze landed on Cora. "Wait with me a moment while the others go in, please."

The choral director gave her a look and then led her charges into the sanctuary. When they were alone, Cora spoke first.

"I'm terribly sorry," she said to the man who had only led this church for a few months. "I tried to explain to the director that I was a terrible choice for the solo."

"No," the reverend said. "You are exactly the right choice." Before she could counter with any of a dozen arguments, he shook his head. "I know who you are, Coraline."

Her breath froze.

"I should explain. We never met back then, but you changed my life."

She blew out a long breath. "I think you've got me mistaken for someone else."

"No," he said again. "We don't have long, so I'll need you to listen without interruption or argument. Once, I had another life before the seminary. You could say I came to the pastorate later in life. This is my first posting. I requested it." He shook his head. "To be more accurate, I begged for it. I wanted to come to Savannah to tell you that if you hadn't sold that restaurant to me, I would probably be dead."

Cora frowned. "I don't follow."

"Oscar's Restaurant, in Manhattan. I wanted that place because a generation ago it belonged to my mother's people. She asked that I get it back, and I was willing to do just about anything to make that happen for her while she was alive. I wasn't the nicest man at the time, so when I say I would have done anything, I think you get my meaning. You see, my last name wasn't always Sanders. I changed it when I entered seminary. Before that, it was Salvaggio."

She looked at him now with new eyes. "Bennie the Butcher Salvaggio?"

He nodded. "My mama told me one night to get on my knees and pray the Lord would forgive me and send me in a different direction. I'd do anything for my mother, but that?" He shrugged. "I promised once I got the restaurant back for her maybe I'd try it. Well, as you know, the place returned to the family."

"I see," Cora whispered.

"And then my mama held me to my promise." He paused to glance around. Outside in the sanctuary, the organ had begun to play. "The Lord met me on my knees in the kitchen of that restaurant. I was never the same since that moment, and now here I am. Unless I wanted my previous reputation to follow me, I figured I'd best find a name that blended in and had no connection to who I used to be."

"It worked," she said. "I had no idea."

"I know," he said. "You were just protecting the man you loved from me. I won't tell you how I got the information, but it's true, isn't it?"

She nodded.

"Well, Cora, I had to tell you this. I wanted to come to Savannah to show you what God did for me, and to tell you that God used you to save me. He's so creative, isn't He?"

"Reverend," she managed, "I have no words."

"No, probably not," he said with a grin, "but you have lyrics. Now I want you to go out there and praise the Lord of miracles, all right? Sing to Him."

She nodded. "I will."

Cora slipped into the choir loft as Reverend Sanders walked into the sanctuary. Her heart was pounding and her mind reeling.

He's so creative, isn't He? Sing to Him.

She smiled. Yes, He was creative. And glorious. And sovereign. Exhaling, she savored every moment of the service. Then it was time for the choral music.

Cora followed the other choir members to center stage. The orchestra that had been rounded up from the local college was placed on one side. As the choir director gave the nod, Cora stepped out of the ranks and into the spotlight.

The opening music rose, and Cora exhaled. Thank You, Lord. I love You so.

"'O holy night, the stars are brightly shining. It is the night of our dear Savior's birth.'"

Everything from that moment until Cora stepped out into the cool night air was a blur. She had sung to the Lord, just as the reverend said.

The reverend formerly known as Bennie the Butcher.

Cora walked home alone, lost in thought, and arrived at the boardinghouse on Oglethorpe Street. Stopping on the sidewalk outside, she smiled.

The building that had stood empty until she arrived almost eight years ago had been filled to the rafters last year due to a fire. It had gradually emptied, first when Miss Havisham declared that she couldn't abide the chaos, and then gradually as refugees found new homes elsewhere.

Tonight they were all back to celebrate. Even Miss Havisham indicated that she would be in attendance.

The candles on the tree twinkled in the front window, and the sound of voices chattering and laughing drifted across the lawn toward her.

Cora knew she should go in. After all, she was the hostess of this Christmas party.

"At least I won't be the last one in."

Cora turned around to see Reverend Sanders standing there. She smiled. "Don't wait for me. I'm enjoying this."

He nodded. "All right, but if you don't come in soon I'll send Miss Havisham after you."

"So you've met my former boarder?"

"I have," he said with a sigh. "She told me she moved because there was a boarder or two whose pasts she found questionable. Imagine if she knew about mine."

They shared a laugh. Then Cora sobered. "No really, go in."

He nodded and walked toward the door. A moment later, he was absorbed into the crowd.

Then a voice startled her. "So, I baked a cake like I promised. I hope you've made dinner."

Cora turned around to see Oscar standing on the sidewalk. True to his word, he was holding what appeared to be a cake.

She ran toward him. Somehow he managed to embrace her without dropping the dessert.

"Merry Christmas, Cora," he told her.

"I'm so glad you're here," she said.

"I told you I'd come back." He looked down at her. "But do you know how much it cost to keep Trask from telling you I was in jail?"

"Stop teasing me," Cora said with a chuckle.

He leaned down to kiss her cheek. "Tomorrow I'll tell you the whole story, but tonight is for celebrating."

Oscar took her by the arm and led her down the walk toward the front door, pausing just long enough to kiss her under the mistletoe.

"Oh," she said a moment before they stepped inside. "We've got a special guest that you'll recognize. Remember Bennie the Butcher?"

Oscar's smile fell. Then he laughed. "You had me going for a minute."

"Like you said. Tonight is for celebrating. Tomorrow I will tell you the whole story. And I expect that stew recipe too."

Chapter Twenty-Seven

SETH AND KENTON STOOD WHEN Julia and Meredith approached the porch. "Seth," Julia said, "you had an appointment tomorrow morning. Couldn't it wait?"

"No," he said, "it couldn't."

"Why not?" Meredith asked.

"I need to come clean with you about something. I've been hoping you'd find Bosco without my telling you, but it's been almost a week."

Julia unlocked the agency door and went to her office, where the makeshift evidence bags were still on her desk. She moved them to the safe and locked them in, then she went into the kitchen to get some drinks.

"Any news about the camera footage?" Meredith joined her. "I've got our client settled and waiting in the conference room."

"Nope," Meredith said as she took three bottles of water and a Diet Dr Pepper from the fridge. "But Carmen took work home. The softy wanted to keep at the search for Bosco. She compared a list of owners of black Dodge trucks to the search for local dog-collar companies. She also unearthed an ad for Travel through Time Tours tours that named their employees. One name made all three lists."

"Really?"

Julia nodded and took two of the bottles from Meredith. "Look at your text."

Meredith put her bottles on the counter and dug in her pocket for her phone. She swiped at the screen and then gasped. "Let's go handle these two and then decide what to do about this."

Both of their phones dinged again, and Julia groaned. "On it," Meredith said.

Juggling all four drinks, Julia barely got through the conference room door before Kenton started talking. "Seth and I have been beating our heads against the wall—"

"Figuratively," Seth interjected. He sighed. "We know Bosco was taken at the tennis courts, but who took him?"

"We know the answer to that," Meredith said as she stepped into the room. She held her phone out to show Julia a text from Carl.

Ed got a pic of Dan Bell with Bosco.

"You should call her," Julia said before turning to Seth and Kenton and handing them each a bottle of water. "Sorry. Go on."

Seth unscrewed the cap on his bottle. "So who took him?"

"Your old nemesis," Julia told him. "The guy you clocked at your reunion."

"Dan Bell?" Seth's jaw went slack and his hand tightened around his water bottle, making some of the water spill out on his hand. "If the police don't do something about him taking Bosco, I will. Enough is enough."

"It won't come to that," Julia said. "But let's get back to my original question. What's so important you had to see us now? And this time I want the specific answer and not the general one."

"Okay," Seth said. "So it all starts with this thing I wanted to do for Amy. She's always changing out Bosco's collars, so I thought, hey, I'll use that as a theme. You know, be creative. So I contacted the guy who made the collars."

"You found out who that was?"

"No," he said. "Sooz was the go-between, but the guy agreed. He did the work and delivered it by courier to Amy with instructions not to open the box."

"Which she did anyway," Julia said.

"Yeah, and I shouldn't be surprised."

"And the present was a collar."

Seth shook his head. "No, it was the contents of the collar. See, each collar had a pocket in it. It was clever design. Unless you knew it was there, you'd never find it. And you could put anything in it—so I ordered a special one."

"And that's why the collar was wider than the nephew's prototypes?"

"Yes," Seth said.

Julia speared him with a look. "So spill. What was in the collar that Dan wanted so badly?"

Kenton looked away as Seth said, "An engagement ring. Let's just say Dan could have retired comfortably if he were to sell it."

"How did you order the collar? Do you have Dan's phone number?" Julia asked

He shook his head. "Like I said, Sooz was the go-between. I had to call her to get to him."

She looked from him to Kenton. "And in spite of all of your resources, neither of you figured out that Dan is Sooz's nephew?"

"We were too busy following all the rabbit trails and dead ends that came in to the tip line," said Kenton, looking sheepish.

Meredith came back into the room. "I called Wally and asked him to meet us there. I suggested that he might want to bring a few of his friends."

"What's happening?" Seth asked.

"We're about to go get Bosco," Julia said. "Want to ride along?"

"Where are we going?"

She slung her purse over her shoulder. "To Dan Bell's house."

Ten minutes later they were standing a half block away from Dan Bell's home. Wally approached them and nodded toward the house. "You're sure?"

Julia pointed to Ed's car as she drove up. "She'll confirm it."

"Who is she?" Wally asked then let out a low whistle when she told him. "Eyewitness is a former fed. I'm satisfied."

Rather than walk immediately toward them, Ed went around to the other side of the car, where Stephanie climbed out. The two women moved quickly to close the distance between them.

Ed wore a grim look. "Stephanie, tell these people what you told me."

Julia could see that Stephanie had been crying. She looked at Ed and then locked eyes with Julia before shifting her attention to Meredith.

"I didn't exactly tell you the truth before." She paused. "See, the part about being paid? That part was true. I was paid."

"By Dan Bell?"

She shrugged. "Yes," she mumbled. "He made a special collar for Amy's dog, and he knew I was the one who always walked Bosco. I guess Mrs. Winter told him."

"So she's involved in this too?"

"Oh, definitely," Stephanie said. "Amy's rich boyfriend had a rock in the hidden pocket of that collar that was worth a fortune. He arranged with Dan to have it made up especially so he could propose. So my job was to watch and see when the dog was walked wearing the collar. That's when I was supposed to get the ring out and give it to him at the park. I wasn't supposed to let go of the leash. That was an accident. I was kneeling down to take the ring out of the collar's hidden pocket when Bosco saw a squirrel."

"So he ran off," Meredith said.

"Yeah, he likes to chase them," Stephanie said. "Dan had to help me catch Bosco. He and Sooz left with the dog, and I called my boss. The next day I had the money under my doormat. By then there was already a big fuss going on about the lost dog, so I figured I'd better take off. I only got as far as Uncle Carl's place. I felt safe there, so I stayed."

"She's willing to testify," Ed told them. "We'll be getting her a lawyer, but Stephanie thought it might help if she told everything up front."

Julia focused on Stephanie. "You did the right thing telling us this."

"And the wrong thing getting involved in a crime." A tear trickled down her cheek.

Wally leaned toward Julia. "Ladies, we need to get this show on the road before the man in that house figures out he's got a welcome party out here and bolts."

"Yes, of course," Julia said. "Come with us, Stephanie."

They moved out of the way. "Go ahead, Wally."

He turned to his officers. "Like we planned." Then he turned back to everyone else. "Civilians, you stay put."

Three minutes later, Dan Bell was in a squad car, and Bosco was cradled in Seth's arms. Julia and Meredith walked over to the open window and waited for the officer to read Bell his rights.

"What?" he spat.

"Was this really all about getting even with Seth?" asked Julia.

"Oh please," he said. "It was about the money. Seth had plenty and I needed some. When Sooz told me who had ordered a collar and what he wanted it for, we hatched the plan. The dog was at her house most of the time, not here. It wasn't until Amy got nosy and sent you over to interrogate Sooz that she moved him here."

"That explains why Amy heard him barking," Meredith said. "Why did you keep the dog? You had the ring."

"We were going to let him go in a couple of days. We were just waiting for the fuss to die down some."

The officer stepped between them. "We're transporting them now."

Julia looked over to see Stephanie being put into a squad car. Wally walked up with a grin as they stepped back to allow the police officer to drive away.

"They'll pick up the aunt too," he told her.

"Thanks for coming, Wally," Meredith said, and then they said their goodbyes.

"Ladies," Seth called, "would you like to see the ring? I've checked, and it's still there. I guess Dan thought if the house was searched the police wouldn't be able to find it."

He held out his hand and showed them the ring. Julia gasped at its beauty. "Amy will love this, Seth," she said.

Seth returned the ring to its hiding place. "Let's go tell Amy that Bosco is home," Julia said.

"I've got a plan for that," he said. "Do you mind?"

"Not at all," she told him. "As long as you don't mind if Meredith and I are there to see him returned."

"I insist on it," he said.

Bosco sat very still in Julia's lap until they reached the bistro. Owing to Amy's new hours, the restaurant was open and the line snaked out the door and down the block in front of Sooz's. A camera crew was covering the event.

When they arrived, Seth phoned Amy and asked her to come outside. Though she argued, eventually she relented. Instantly she was ambushed by a reporter who stuck a microphone in her face as the lights went on.

"Sweet," Seth said. "This is better than I could have planned."

He stepped out of the car with Kenton parting the crowd. When they were a few paces from Amy, Seth knelt down and released Bosco, who made a beeline for his owner.

Amy squealed and picked up her beloved pup then embraced Seth. A moment later, when she was distracted by the reporter's question, Seth dropped to one knee.

"Amy," he said over the noise of the crowd that had begun to clap, "will you marry me?"

Amy gasped and placed her hands over her mouth. "Yes!"

"Awesome," Seth said, "but you'll have to get the ring from Bosco."

Later Meredith and Julia sat in the empty restaurant with a beaming Seth and Amy. Bosco was curled up in Amy's lap. Kenton wanted to be there when Wally made the arrest of Sooz Winter, so he'd bid them an early goodbye after a heartfelt congratulations. Then later, he reported back with the details.

The phone rang, and Amy moved across the room to answer.

Seth shook his head. "All of that just to make money. Such greed. I can't believe that anyone would put money and things over people and pets. It just baffles me that—"

"Seth," Amy called from the staircase, "I hope you mean what you're saying right now."

"Why's that, honey?" he asked with a smile.

"Remember that Julia Child recipe card that you bought for me?"

Seth's smile went south. "Yes."

"Again," she said as she stepped into view with Bosco in one arm and the remains of the protective case that had once held the very expensive gift from her fiancé.

Seth rose and let out a long breath. Then he turned to Amy. This time his smile was broad and swift. "I mean every single word. Now toss that mess into the trash and let's go turn on the television. It's just about time to watch our proposal on the evening news."

"That's our cue to go," Meredith said.

"No, stay please," Seth said.

"Is it true that you planned all of that down to the television crew?" Amy asked Seth as they climbed the stairs to her apartment.

"As far as you know," he told her. He looked down at Bosco. "I won't tell if you won't."

Dear Reader,

I hope you've enjoyed this visit to Savannah. I have to admit that it is one of the most beautiful cities I've ever visited, and I have traveled extensively. Recently my husband and I celebrated our tenth anniversary by spending time there. Our hotel was once part of the Citadel, and the view out our window was of a square that was once a parade ground for cadets.

There was so much to be inspired by in Savannah. A restaurant we visited on our first night there was situated in an old church overlooking the city market and had the entire text of Sun Tsu's *The Art of War* written by hand on the ceiling. Another restaurant— are you sensing a theme for our visit?—was located in an old home on Oglethorpe Street that became the inspiration for Cora's boardinghouse.

Savannah's lush green squares were laid out in the city's original plan and are still tended with care today. In writing this book—and while visiting the city—I tried to bring as many of the squares, parks, and other sites as I could into the story. The most fun was standing at the edge of Forsyth Park and photographing the actual building that is the model for the Magnolia Investigations offices!

I was so tempted to ring the bell and ask for Julia or Meredith or Carmen.

A visit to Savannah is a trip through a genteel present, a storied past, and a bright future. From the busy riverfront to the fountain at Forsyth Square, there is so much to love about the city. I hope you go there soon, and if you do, tell Julia, Meredith, and Carmen hello for me.

Enjoy!

Signed,
Kathleen Y'Barbo

About the Author

KATHLEEN Y'BARBO IS A MULTIPLE Carol Award and RITA nominee and bestselling author of more than one hundred books with over two million copies of her books in print in the US and abroad. A tenth-generation Texan and certified paralegal, she is a member of the Texas Bar Association Paralegal Division, Texas A&M Association of Former Students, and the Texas A&M Women Former Students (Aggie Women), Texas Historical Society, Novelists Inc., and American Christian Fiction Writers. She would also be a member of the Daughters of the American Republic, Daughters of the Republic of Texas, and a few others if she would just remember to fill out the paperwork that Great-Aunt Mary Beth has sent her more than once.

Kathleen and her hero-in-combat-boots husband have their own surprise love story that unfolded on social media a few years back. They now make their home just north of Houston, Texas, and are the parents and in-laws of a blended family of Texans, Okies, and a family of very adorable Londoners.

To find out more about Kathleen or connect with her through social media, check out her website at kathleenybarbo.com.

The Truth Behind the Fiction

The Great Savannah Races

WHEN OSCAR COMES TO THE door of Cora's boardinghouse, he is greeted with the question of whether he is one of those race car drivers. In 1908, Savannah was the host city for the first of what was termed the Great Savannah Races, a precursor of the Formula One races that are still held today. This race was the culmination of efforts by the Savannah Automobile Club. The race's official name was the International Grand Prize Race of the Automobile Club of America.

On March 18 and 19 of that year, automobile drivers from all over the world gathered there to compete in that first ever Savannah event. The racecourse was twenty-five miles in length and laid out all over the city. Mayor George Tiedman declared a city holiday so the citizens could all come out and cheer on the participants. Louis Wagner won the inaugural race driving a Fiat.

Races continued to be held in Savannah annually through 1911. In that year, the event attracted the largest crowds ever as they witnessed the Vanderbilt Cup race. This race, with a length of two hundred ninety-one miles, was the fastest of the competition when the winner crossed the finish line with a time of three hours and fifty-six minutes.

A marker honoring the Grand Prize Race was put in place in 1955 on Waters Avenue at the site where the grandstands once stood. To find out more about the Great Savannah Races, check out the Great Savannah Race Museum at 411 Abercorn Street. The museum is open by appointment. Call 912-398-4785 for more information.

CORA'S CARDAMOM CAKE

Ingredients:

1⅓ cups softened butter

1⅔ cups sugar

4 eggs

1 cup milk

2½ cups all-purpose flour

3 teaspoons baking powder

5 teaspoons cardamom

(or more to taste)

Directions:

Preheat oven to 350 degrees. Grease and flour a bundt pan and set aside.

Cream butter and sugar then add the eggs, one at a time, mixing well after each addition. Mix together dry ingredients and pour into wet ingredients, being careful not to overmix. Pour into cake pan and tap the pan to release any air bubbles.

Bake for one hour or until golden brown. Let cake cool for ten minutes in the pan before turning onto a rack to cool completely.

*Read on for a sneak peek of another exciting book
in the Savannah Secrets series!*

Honeybees & Legacies

BY SHAEN LAYLE

MEREDITH BELLEFONTAINE FANNED THE NECK of her blouse to cool
off as she strolled along East Taylor Street. It was the beginning of
September in Savannah, but it still felt like the middle of summer. A
few more months' time would provide a respite from the sticky
Southern humidity that turned her curls into frizz quicker than you
could say "fried green tomato," but for now, the weather remained
warm. At least she was spending Saturday with two of her favorite
people.

"Gran, where are we going now?"

Meredith glanced over at her granddaughter, Kinsley. The blond
ten-year-old's cheeks were rosy from walking, and a wide smile
graced her delicate features. Her glittered T-shirt and ruffled sneakers perfectly conveyed her youthful attitude.

Meredith smiled. "Our next stop is just up ahead." She turned to
her grandson. At eleven, Kaden was nearly as tall as Meredith and
looked every inch a newly minted preteen. He'd even gotten braces
a few weeks ago, though he appeared uneasy with his mouthful of

mumbling metal. "Quiz time, Kaden. Whose monument do we find in Monterey Square?"

The morning's walk served two purposes. Sure, it allowed her to clock precious time with her grandchildren. She'd never turn that down. But it also served as a history lesson. She had already presented them with some national history, as the three of them had attended an early morning Remembrance Ceremony for 9/11 in J.F. Gregory Park. Even though the attacks had happened long before Kaden or Kinsley had been born, Meredith felt it was important to share the details of that day with her grandchildren.

Now it was time for some local history. The squares of Savannah—twenty-two out of twenty-four still intact—told the story of the city better than any textbook. Since Kaden was trying out for his school's newly formed Quiz Bowl team, he needed to brush up on Georgia history. "Whose monument do we find in Monterey Square?" she prompted again.

Kaden blew a breath past his braces. "I don't know. Why don't you tell me?"

His tone held a bitter edge. It was unlike him, and it worried Meredith. Kaden's father—who was Meredith's oldest son, Carter—had mentioned that Kaden was having a tough time adjusting to middle school. He'd insisted it wasn't a big deal, though, and hadn't wanted to discuss the particulars.

Meredith understood. Boys on the cusp of adolescence needed privacy and respect, something she grasped as she'd raised two boys of her own. Complicating matters was the fact that Kaden also had high-functioning autism. It was a real struggle for him to convey emotions.

She wanted to help him, though. She was his grandmother. Concern for his well-being was practically written into the job description. Maybe if she approached things in a roundabout way, she could get at the root of the problem. "Not too excited about school on a Saturday, kiddo?"

Kaden swung his freckled face toward her but didn't answer her question directly. "Can we go straight to the Farmer's Market? I don't want to learn any more history."

"Why not?" Meredith tried to keep her tone light and encouraged Kinsley to run ahead as they closed in on Monterey Square. Meredith could see the points of its Casimir Pulaski monument peeking through the still-green leaves of the live oaks.

"Because I don't need to know Georgia history." Kaden bit off the sentence. "I'm not trying out for Quiz Bowl. Didn't Dad tell you?"

Meredith studied him. Was this the same boy who, on their last visit, had delightedly rattled off every piece of information he could remember about the golden orb spider? Kaden had always been so enthusiastic about school…until this year. If she'd hoped to provide a listening ear for him, things weren't going well so far.

"No, he didn't say anything. Why aren't you trying out?"

"I just—I just don't want to." Kaden balled his hands into fists.

"Any particular reason for that?"

"No. Can we drop this?" Kaden hung his head, looking defeated.

Meredith exhaled. It was possible Kaden was just dealing with the emotional turbulence of adolescence, but somehow, she sensed there was more to the situation than that. She decided to try a different tactic. "Okay, we'll bypass Monterey Square for now."

Kinsley skipped back to Meredith. "Aw, I wanted to see the monument."

Meredith squinted up at the marble structure as they passed. It was interesting, with a miniature Lady Liberty on top and a bronze relief of the Revolutionary War hero, Pulaski, below. History was one of her passions, and she'd been excited to share her knowledge with her grandchildren. But it would have to wait. Today wasn't about her. It was about Kaden and about what he needed.

Meredith pushed aside her own feelings, as she teasingly tugged Kinsley's ponytail. "The Farmer's Market will be fun too. I just might buy a yummy apple pie…and then eat it for lunch."

"The whole thing? By yourself? Can I have dessert for lunch?" Kinsley grinned, acting as if she liked the idea. It probably wasn't the healthiest option, but they'd had green smoothies for breakfast, and according to Meredith's pedometer, they'd chalked up a lot of steps already. A small treat wouldn't hurt, as long as they kept things in balance.

"I think we could arrange that. Hopefully, your father won't have my hide for it. If he does, I'll have to plead Grandparent's Privileges in *loco parentis*."

She hoped the dramatic offer of pie for lunch would coax Kaden from his cocoon, but he only pulled his shoulders in tighter. His coolness pricked her feelings, and her heart ached for him. If only she could find the right words to get him to open up.

The Farmer's Market was at the south end of Forsyth Park. Instead of cutting through the green space, which was crowded with locals and tourists alike, they took Whitaker Street around the perimeter. The new route wasn't as shaded, but it did allow them to pass by Magnolia Investigations, where Meredith worked with her longtime friend, Julia Foley, as a private investigator. It had been Meredith's husband's agency before he passed away, and Ron had prided himself on building a business that had helped many people in the Savannah area. She hoped to carry on the legacy now that he'd begun years before.

"Can we stop by your work? Please?" Kinsley piped up beside Meredith. The little girl was fascinated with Meredith's job, though Meredith had already had several lengthy conversations with her, assuring her that the reality wasn't quite as glamorous as it looked in the movies.

In fact, if Meredith was being honest, the reality lately had been a little concerning. At a week and a half into September, business had been unusually slow. No, worse than that. Completely dead. If the trend continued, they could be in real trouble. Magnolia Investigations needed a new case soon, and they needed a substantial one. Meredith kept her concerns to herself, though, as she ruffled Kinsley's hair.

"Not today, sweetheart. Maybe next time you visit?"

Kinsley brightened. "Like next Thursday?"

Meredith laughed. "No, not next Thursday. You two have school, silly girl. Or did you forget?"

"No, we don't." Kinsley looked triumphant. "Mom said we're on vacation then."

At Meredith's confused expression, Kaden explained. "Fall break starts Thursday. I can't wait."

The intensity of his voice set off Meredith's internal grandma alarms again. She didn't say anything, though, just pressed her lips together tightly.

"So, can we?" Kinsley asked.

"Can you what? Visit next week?" Meredith hedged with giving an answer. As much as she adored spending time with her grand-kids, the timing for an extended visit wasn't ideal. She really needed to put some effort into reaching some new clients. If anything, she needed to be working more, not less.

Kinsley looked at her expectantly.

Meredith took a deep breath. "I'd love to have you visit, sweetie… but we'll have to talk to your mom and dad about it before we make any definite plans. Okay?"

"Awesome! I know they'll say yes." Kinsley jumped and pumped her fists to show her excitement. Kaden offered a tight smile at his sister's exuberant display.

They walked the rest of the way in silence, soon entering the shade of the park. The buzz of conversations filled the air. Multicolored tents stretched over tables that lined the length of the walkways. It seemed to Meredith as if the market grew larger every year. She couldn't wait to drift from booth to booth, examining all the fruits, vegetables, jams, relishes, and baked goods.

"Gran, look! They do have apple pies." Kinsley pointed a fin-ger at a nearby table, just as Meredith's phone rang from her pocket.

She slid it out and glanced at the screen. It was her good friend, Maggie Lu. Maggie Lu didn't technically work for Magnolia Investigations, but she rivaled Meredith's knowledge of Savannah history and had assisted her and Julia on cases many times before.

A flicker of hope sprang up in Meredith. Maybe Maggie Lu was calling about a possible case now. She'd directed clients to the agency before.

Meredith pressed a few bills into her granddaughter's hand. "Why don't you buy us some pies?" Kinsley beamed and ran ahead. Meredith nudged Kaden, who still stood mutely at her side. "Keep an eye on her, okay? I'll catch up in a minute."

Kaden nodded, a serious expression still glued to his face, and plodded up the path after his sister.

Meredith answered the call. "Hi, Maggie Lu."

Maggie Lu's warm, full voice filled the receiver. "Sorry to bother you on a weekend, but I wanted to see if you were free next Sunday."

Meredith exhaled a breath. Maggie Lu wasn't calling about a potential case, then. It was more likely a "surprise" for her birthday, which fell on the twentieth. Her friends had been hinting about a party for weeks. She didn't let on to Maggie Lu about her suspicions, though, and kept her tone light. "I think I'm free then. Any particular reason why you're asking?"

"You'll find out," Maggie Lu said mysteriously. "Where are you anyway? Sounds louder than a nestful of hornets."

Meredith laughed, still keeping an eye on Kaden and Kinsley, who had queued up at a nearby booth and were waiting patiently for pies. "I'm at the Farmer's Market. It's packed."

"At the Farmer's Market…," Maggie Lu said slowly. "Hey, could I ask you for a tiny favor?"

"Of course."

"Could you pick me up a few jars of honey? It's for Charlene. She's working with Maribelle to dream up some new fall recipes for the restaurant." Maggie Lu's daughter, Charlene, was the owner of the Downhome Diner, one of Meredith's favorite restaurants in Savannah's historic district.

"Sure, I can do that." Meredith finished up her conversation with Maggie Lu then scanned the park for vendors selling honey. A booth directly ahead sported a banner with a picture of a honeybee on it. CHARLIE BEE HONEY. Perfect. She caught Kaden's eye from across the square and made a big, dramatic show of pointing at the Charlie Bee sign so he'd know where she was headed.

Then she turned her attention to the vendor's charming booth. A long line snaked in front of the table. Apparently, other people thought Charlie Bee sounded perfect too. She considered skipping the booth altogether and scouting for another vendor. If people were willing to wait at this place, though, it must mean the merchandise was worth it. She slipped to the back of the line and killed time by studying Charlie Bee's wares.

Jars of honey glistened like amber in the sunlight. Meredith scanned the labels. She'd had no idea there were so many different varieties. Honey infused with orange blossom, lavender, wildflowers. Even an intriguing type called "winter white" that looked like whipped cream.

She was also delighted to discover that the booth sold more than just honey. Painted canvases of local Savannah landmarks were propped up on easels. Whoever had created them had done a fine job of capturing the energy and feel of the city. Meredith was so absorbed in studying the artwork that she didn't even notice that the crowd in front of her had cleared out.

"These paintings are beautiful," she told the woman running the booth. Her name tag read NIKKI WILLIAMS. She looked every inch an artist, from her funky head wrap to the multicolored beads strung around her neck.

"It's something I enjoy." Nikki graciously shrugged off the compliment. "Would you like to try a sample of honey?" She held out a tiny plastic spoon to Meredith.

The sample Nikki offered was delicious, light and flowery with none of the cloying sweetness Meredith had come to expect with store-bought honey. She started to drop the empty spoon into the trash, but as she did, something hit her on the wrist. Was it a bug? She waved her hands to shoo it away.

Nikki looked embarrassed. "I'm so sorry." She glanced at the table next to them. It was another honey booth, though not nearly as well populated as Charlie Bee. A little girl sat in a chair beside her mother, kicking her legs. A mischievous look lit her eyes as she reached behind her and pulled a long stem of yellow foxtail from the ground. In plain view of Meredith and Nikki, she shot another foxtail head onto Nikki's table, which nearly landed in the open jar of honey from which Nikki provided samples.

"Angela?" Nikki addressed the girl's mother, but the woman didn't look up from endlessly scrolling on her phone.

"I'm so sorry. Excuse me for a second." Nikki walked over to the neighboring booth. She spoke quietly to the woman about her daughter's unruly behavior.

Angela, however, seemed unconcerned. She halfheartedly scolded the girl before leaning her cheek onto her fist again, blocking out her view of Nikki's booth. Within seconds, the girl began shooting foxtail heads onto Nikki's table again. This time, Nikki just took a deep breath and ignored the situation.

After sampling different varieties of honey, Meredith chose several jars that she thought Charlene would like. Nikki started to wrap them up but stopped as her cell phone began playing a ringtone. She sighed heavily as she glanced at the screen. "Oh no..."

She snuck another glance at Angela before placing the cell phone facedown. Then she hurriedly finished bagging Meredith's purchase and raised her voice to the group of eager shoppers who had congregated behind Meredith. "I'm sorry, everyone. I have to close up shop early. Emergency at home."

Meredith heard a few scattered groans from the line behind her before people started to disperse. Several of the customers queued up in front of the neighboring honey booth. Angela cast a sideways glance at Nikki packing up her table and looked pleased.

Meredith searched Nikki's face. "Is everything all right?"

"Not really." Nikki hastily loaded her merchandise and signage into a folding wheeled cart. "I just got an app notification that my beehives have been tampered with."

Meredith was intrigued. "There's an app for that?"

Nikki nodded. "I get an alert any time the weight of the beehive shifts."

"How fascinating."

"More like frustrating. Even though it looks like only one box was damaged, I could still lose my swarm." Nikki tore down her storefront banner and shoved it into the cart too. She lowered her voice. Worry was evident in her eyes. "I just don't know why somebody would do this."

"What makes you think it was an intentional attack? Couldn't a hive accidentally fall over?"

"Not unless there was a hurricane across town that I don't know about." Nikki gave a wry smile. "The hives weigh fifty pounds each. They don't just tumble over without help."

"You should call the police."

"I plan to as soon as I get to the car, but I don't know if they'll be able to help me. Several of my friend's hives were vandalized last year, and the police weren't able to do much." Nikki frowned, deepening the crease between her eyebrows.

A damaged beehive certainly wasn't the substantial case Meredith had envisioned taking on, but she did truly feel for Nikki and wanted to help her. Meredith dug in her purse for a business card for Magnolia Investigations and slid it across the table to Nikki. "I hope the police will be able to help you. If not, though, feel free to give me a call. Maybe I can do something."

Nikki scanned the words on the card before turning to Meredith with wide eyes. "You'd take on a case that small? I guess I assumed private investigators only dealt with large crimes, like…embezzlement or something."

"Not always." Meredith laughed. It seemed Kinsley wasn't the only person who had misconceptions about the nature of her work. "We'd be happy to look into your case."

"Thank you so much." Nikki waved goodbye then exited the park.

Meredith left the now-empty booth to track down Kaden and Kinsley. Kinsley had already scarfed down half of her pie, though Kaden, still sporting a glum expression, hadn't touched his.

"Here, Gran." He handed her a fistful of change, as well as a bag which contained her dessert. But Meredith's mind was firmly fixed on other matters, and they extended far beyond pie.

The agency might have some new work, but was chasing down beehive vandals the kind of case Magnolia Investigations needed to be taking on right now?

A Note from the Editors

WE HOPE YOU ENJOY THE Savannah Secrets series, created by the Books and Inspirational Media Division of Guideposts, a nonprofit organization that touches millions of lives every day through products and services that inspire, encourage, help you grow in your faith, and celebrate God's love in every aspect of your daily life.

Thank you for making a difference with your purchase of this book, which helps fund our many outreach programs to military personnel, prisons, hospitals, nursing homes, and educational institutions. To learn more, visit GuidepostsFoundation.org.

We also maintain many useful and uplifting online resources. Visit Guideposts.org to read true stories of hope and inspiration, access OurPrayer network, sign up for free newsletters, download free e-books, join our Facebook community, and follow our stimulating blogs.

To learn about other Guideposts publications, including the bestselling devotional *Daily Guideposts*, go to ShopGuideposts.org, call (800) 932-2145, or write to Guideposts, PO Box 5815, Harlan, Iowa 51593.

Sign up for the
Guideposts Fiction Newsletter
and stay up-to-date on the books you love!

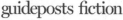

You'll get sneak peeks of new releases, recommendations from other Guideposts readers, and special offers just for you . . . *and it's FREE!*

Just go to Guideposts.org/Newsletters today to sign up.

Guideposts.

Visit Guideposts.org/Shop or call (800) 932-2145

Find more inspiring stories in these best-loved Guideposts fiction series!

Mysteries of Lancaster County

Follow the Classen sisters as they unravel clues and uncover hidden secrets in Mysteries of Lancaster County. As you get to know these women and their friends, you'll see how God brings each of them together for a fresh start in life.

Secrets of Wayfarers Inn

Retired schoolteachers find themselves owners of an old warehouse-turned-inn that is filled with hidden passages, buried secrets, and stunning surprises that will set them on a course to puzzling mysteries from the Underground Railroad.

Tearoom Mysteries Series

Mix one stately Victorian home, a charming lakeside town in Maine, and two adventurous cousins with a passion for tea and hospitality. Add a large scoop of intriguing mystery, and sprinkle generously with faith, family, and friends, and you have the recipe for *Tearoom Mysteries*.

Ordinary Women of the Bible

Richly imagined stories—based on facts from the Bible—have all the plot twists and suspense of a great mystery, while bringing you fascinating insights on what it was like to be a woman living in the ancient world.

To learn more about these books, visit Guideposts.org/Shop